So Proudly She Sailed

Tales of
OLD IRONSIDES

So Proudly She Sailed

Tales of OLD IRONSIDES

by Olga Cabral

Illustrated with photographs

HOUGHTON MIFFLIN COMPANY
BOSTON 1981

Library of Congress Cataloging in Publication Data

Cabral, Olga.
So proudly she sailed.

Summary: A fictionalized account of the U.S.S. Constitution's many voyages from her launching in 1797 to her last restoration more than a century later.
1. Constitution (Frigate)—Juvenile fiction.
[1. Constitution (Frigate)—Fiction] I. Title.
PZ7.C113So   [Fic]   81-6465
ISBN 0-395-31670-7   AACR2

Contents

Introduction ix

PART ONE

Chapter I "She Moves! She Lives!" *1*
Chapter II Off the Spanish Main *15*
Chapter III To the Shores of Tripoli *25*
Chapter IV Yankee Schoolboys *36*
Chapter V Viking's Death of the *Philadelphia* *47*
Chapter VI Battle of Tripoli Bay *58*

PART TWO

Chapter VII Mutiny! *73*
Chapter VIII Mr. Madison's War *83*
Chapter IX Hounds of the Sea *95*
Chapter X "Old Ironsides" *105*
Chapter XI Home of the Brave *113*

PART THREE

Chapter XII Saved by a Poet *127*
Chapter XIII Mad Jack and the Mandarins *131*
Chapter XIV Black Market in Ebony *147*
Chapter XV The Last Big Crossing *159*

Afterword 169

So Proudly She Sailed

Tales of
OLD IRONSIDES

Introduction

*T*HIS IS the story of a ship.

To sailors, a ship is always "she." And perhaps it is a little strange that a ship should be referred to as a living person.

And yet it is not so strange. For to sailors ships *are* living beings. A ship has a soul, a character, and a personality. She mothers the crew aboard her, brings them home safely through storm, adventure, and danger. They grow to love her and speak affectionately of her.

The ship in this story was a frigate, a wooden man-of-war. She was born when the country was very young, when George Washington, Thomas Jefferson, Tom Paine, and all their fellow patriots were still alive.

She was a ship of sail, every plank and beam of her lovingly made by hand. Her flag, fifteen stars and fifteen stripes, was made by Mrs. Betsy Ross. Her bolts and sheathing were made by the Boston coppersmith, Mr.

Paul Revere. Her masts were like pine trees, her sails like summer clouds. Her power was the wind, and the sailors who climbed her ropes and rigging had skills that are now forgotten.

They christened her the *Constitution*. In a great battle she won another name — *Old Ironsides*. Her wooden sides were made of oak that was tough as iron, and they rebuffed the enemy's cannonballs, letting them glance off harmlessly, as though she scorned to take notice of them.

She fought famous battles and grew too old for war. In her peaceful days she was a relief ship in the Greek war of independence. She visited the China seas, chased slave traders off the African coast, and ferried a steam engine across to Europe. In an age when sailing ships were beginning to disappear from the ocean, she circled the globe by way of bleak Cape Horn, like Magellan and the old mariners. She sailed on every ocean and traveled half a million miles in her active lifetime.

She was condemned once, and saved by a poet. She was then overhauled, repaired, and put to work once more. Again she grew old and was condemned as a useless old hulk, to be towed out to sea and sunk. But the people would not let her grow old or die. This time school children helped save the historic old ship.

To restore her exactly as she was in the days of her battle with the *Guerrière* required almost a million dollars. For by this time there was nothing sound enough to patch. She was, in fact, a mass of crumbling and wormy old oak — a mere shell.

Congress appropriated part of the money but the biggest share was raised by the people themselves. All over the country, children brought their pennies to school for the fund to save *Old Ironsides*. Much of the money was contributed by them.

Dusty archives were consulted and old plans pored over. There were great difficulties, however, in the way of restoring her.

First of all, the giant white oaks were now extinct. It took a two-year search to locate some old trees, cut fifty years before and lying in a pond, that were of the proper grade and tremendous size required.

It was no less difficult to find proper workmen — men who still knew the art of wooden shipbuilding. The country was combed for old craftsmen with forgotten skills — ship fasteners, dubbers, plank hewers, bevelers.

But all difficulties were finally overcome. In 1931, completely restored to the condition of her youth, *Old Ironsides* sailed again on a triumphant tour of the seaports of America, passing through the Panama Canal and going as far north on the Pacific coast as the state of Washington.

Now she is a very old lady, dreaming out her days in Boston, where she was born. They say there is little of the original ship left, she has been repaired so many times. Maybe not more than 10 percent of the old *Constitution*.

Perhaps this small fraction is her heart. At any rate, there is enough of it left to dream and remember the old days, the days of "wooden ships and iron men."

Perhaps she remembers the hundreds upon hundreds of sailors — and small boys, too — who served upon her decks; some of whose stories make up her story; some of whose lives make up her long lifetime . . .

Part One

CHAPTER I

"She Moves! She Lives!"

*A*T DAWN on October 21, 1797, the sound of a cannon awoke the good people of Boston.

It woke Johnny Griggs, a "bound boy" asleep on a straw pallet in an attic near the harbor.

Johnny was dreaming when the cannon went off. The house shook and the windows rattled as he opened his eyes. The sound of the cannon fitted in so beautifully with what he had been dreaming that he couldn't quite get his bearings. The straw pallet was a deck, the attic room a ship, and the floor trembled because of the roll and sway of the sea. The sea was in the room, and it swirled about Johnny in long, cold, hissing waves.

When he looked around, he saw, instead of the sea, the low, dark loft and the small square window where the chill dawn looked in.

"Jiminy!" he gasped, and woke up fully.

For this was no ordinary day. The new frigate was

going to be launched. The cannon was the signal to the people of Boston that on this day, the day of her birth, the *Constitution* would float on the sea at high tide, at noon.

Quickly, Johnny reached for his clothes and pulled them to him under the warm blankets. From the shop below a broom handle rapped upon the ceiling, and Mr. Jedidiah Moss yelled his usual morning greeting: "Be ye alive up there, boy?"

"I'm acoming!" Johnny yelled back, and rolled out of his cozy bed. He thumped about noisily in the chill gloom, getting into his stockings with holes, boots that were too large, frayed trousers, and jacket worn cheese-cloth-thin at the elbows. A moment or two later he dashed out into the street and sloshed his face with icy water from the rain barrel.

Johnny was an immigrant boy whose parents had died on the terrible crossing from Liverpool to the New World. He could remember it vividly — it had all happened only two years ago. The people had been packed in like herring, the food had rotted and the water had been foul and wormy, and almost a third of the passengers had died.

When he landed in Boston, Johnny was an orphan. Mr. and Mrs. Jedidiah Moss bought the lad from the ship's captain, to serve until he was twenty-one years old in order to work out his parents' passage and his own. The Mosses were penny pinchers who kept a wigmaker's shop, and their dispositions were further soured by the fact that nowadays wigs and other such refinements were going out of style.

"You, Johnny!" scolded Mrs. Moss from inside the shop. "No daydreaming now! There're chores aplenty to be done! And you'll not set foot out of this house until they're done proper!"

"Yes'm," said Johnny. The water was icy cold, the street dark and gloomy, but he made no move to hurry inside.

One by one, in all the windows of Boston, candlelight appeared. The town had never been lit up so early in the morning. Down by the harbor there was music — drums and fifes, bursts of singing, parades.

Johnny's legs twitched, especially when the cobbler's boy apprentice burst out of the shop next door, waved his cap at Johnny, and yelled, "Hi! I got the day off! Hurry up — yer're missing the best of it!"

But though this was a big day for all of Boston, Johnny had not been given a holiday by the Mosses. He had to stay indoors and sweep and scrub and do dull chores while the streets got livelier and livelier with people flocking to the harbor.

When Johnny was finally given his freedom, the harbor was jammed. People had come from all the nearby towns and hamlets. Never had he seen so many people at Boston harbor, or so many ships. There were more big ships than Johnny could count — ships with high black hulls and castled decks, ships from across the world's seas, recognized by the flags they flew as Dutchmen, black and weatherbeaten East Indiamen, Spaniards, and Frenchmen, as well as every kind of sloop, brig, schooner, fishing boat, and rowboat bobbing about on the chill, choppy sea.

The new frigate, the *Constitution*, stood poised on the ship's ways, ready for launching. For two years the people of Boston had watched her grow into a stately ship under the hammers and saws of workmen and artisans. Her black hull, curving like a pair of wings, was shiny with new paint. She had a white ribbon painted around her gun deck, and from this her hull tapered upward and inward to the spar deck, giving her a fine, symmetrical line. Like other Bostoners, Johnny felt an affectionate pride in the beautiful frigate, just as if he too owned some tiny share of her.

He tried to wriggle his way through the crowd, catching the drifts of talk. A pockmarked sailor with golden earrings said that now the frigate would be sailing to fight the Barbary pirates and teach them a lesson. A shopkeeper in conservative smallclothes and silver buckles said that talk was cheap and that the young country should not fight anyone just now — it had too many enemies at sea, and trouble enough at home, too. The pockmarked sailor retorted that Yankee ships needed freedom of the seas to travel in search of trade, to which the shopkeeper rejoined that a navy was just a waste of the people's money and it would be cheaper to keep on paying tribute to the pirates.

When the sailor hotly replied that the country's new navy, with its three ships, would do the job that the mighty fleets of Lord Nelson and Napoleon hadn't been able to do, Johnny piped up with, "Huroo! I say so, too!"

The gentleman in smallclothes angrily pushed Johnny and disdainfully drew off. But no one paid any more attention to him. There was a surge of movement in the crowd.

Aboard the frigate, a man was hastily running up the flag. With fifteen stars and fifteen stripes, it whipped from the top of the lofty mast. The crowd burst out cheering.

The man who had raised the flag clambered up on the rigging and waved his cap. He was no uniformed notable in gold braid and cocked hat, though. A workingman in rough homespuns, he had no right to be there. Now there was a great outcry. Half-a-dozen soldiers ran to arrest the man, who had usurped the honor that had been awaiting Captain Nicholson. But the workman slipped over the side and with agile legs disappeared in the cheering crowd.

"That's Sam Bentley!" cried an artisan in a leather apron. "He bet me last night he'd be the first to run up her flag. Said no one had more right than a workman who helped build her. And he did it, too! Ha-ha! Now look at the cap'n! He's fair hopping!''

The captain, a pompous-looking martinet, had just arrived at the scene, only to find that the ceremony was already over. The flag had been raised without him, and by a plain workingman at that. The crowd seemed to relish the joke. There was nothing for Captain Nicholson to do then but make the best of it. He gave the signal for the launching to begin.

The crowd pushed and surged, trying to get closer to hear the speeches. But Johnny could not see or hear anything. He tried to get onto a wharf, but a watchman with a cane chased him. A great many small boats were about, and Johnny looked at them wistfully.

Two sailors rowed close to the wharf. One had a red beard that glittered in the sun and a fell of red hair upon his sunburned arms. Johnny begged to be taken aboard. The two sailors looked at one another and shrugged. Then the red-bearded one, who was doing the rowing, pulled over.

"Hop in, then," he said. "You'll help us bail."

The water was rough and kept sloshing over the sides. The wind felt cold and raw, but Johnny didn't mind. From the water he now had a clear view of the frigate.

"Well," said Red Beard gruffly, "she'll soon be signing on a crew. Going to ship out on her, lad?"

"Me?" Johnny cried. His heart skipped a beat or two.

Red Beard nodded. "She's a man-of-war. She'll be needing gunners, like myself. And small lads like yourself, to keep the guns fed. How about it, mate? Will you ship with Jethro Stubbs and go to fight the Barbary pirates?"

A great smile spread over Johnny's face. In wonderment and delight, he considered this invitation to a dazzling future. And then he remembered the wigmaker who owned him. Crestfallen, he said, "I'm a bound boy. I've got no rights. I've got to work out my time."

"Aye?" said Jethro Stubbs. He looked at Johnny keenly. "Well, so was I once."

"Look!" the other sailor cried, pointing toward the frigate. "She's being launched!"

All along the ways carpenters with big hammers began knocking out the huge wedges that held the *Constitution*. As the wedges fell away one by one, there was a creaking sound. The frigate stirred, seemed to tremble and to take a deep breath before her plunge into life. The carpenters threw aside their hammers and leaped out of the way as her towering black hull slid forward. Faster and faster she slid. Then, with a great splash, she hit the sea.

"She moves! She lives!" cried Jethro Stubbs.

She floated clear as the shore cannon saluted her. A schooner strung with little flags and bright streamers moved to tow her to her anchorage. The ringing of churchbells and the wild cheering of the dense crowds along the waterfront rolled back in waves, and over it all sounded the boom of cannon announcing to the whole world that the *Constitution* was safely launched.

The notables in the pavilion were standing, watching her move slowly away. There stood Mr. John Adams, the President of the United States, resplendent in gold lace. And the aging coppersmith who had made all the ship's copperwork, Mr. Paul Revere, muffled in a scarlet-lined cloak against the chill wind. And Colonel Claghorne, the frigate's builder. And Mr. Joshua Humphreys, her designer. And many others.

"Now it's all over," said Jethro Stubbs. He looked at Johnny shivering in his wet clothes. "Back with you now, matey. You're fair drenched to the skin, and like as not'll catch a whipping for it."

In the months that followed, Johnny did take many a hiding for his stolen moments on the wharves. Whenever he could he would go down to the waterfront to look at the frigate. That was not too often, because the Mosses considered idleness the product of the devil. Old Jedidiah Moss could tell almost to the minute how long a given errand ought to take. And the law gave a master the right to whip a servant.

Johnny kept looking for the red-bearded sailor at the waterfront taverns. But sailors came and went — rough, boisterous men with wind-tanned faces and the free, open manners of the sea. In his loafing moments Johnny looked into many faces, but he could not find his lost friend. The frigate seemed to have no need of a crew anyway. He thought she was never going to sail.

Then her guns arrived from England. They were big twenty-four-pounders. The frigate's decks rang with the sound of hammers as the guns were mounted on their wooden carriages. Her spars were set and her complicated rigging strung. Johnny could peer inside the Old Granary Building and watch the sailmakers sewing her suit of sails. They sat cross-legged like tailors amid acres of white canvas, using padded leather palms in place of thimbles, and huge needles.

She *was* going to sail, at last!

But not against the Barbary pirates. Congress, it seemed, preferred to keep right on bribing them. There was now a new enemy — Napoleonic France. French privateers were spoiling the West Indies trade, cutting off one of the young nation's lifelines. Not North Africa but the Spanish Main was the frigate's destination.

Johnny had stopped looking for the sailor Jethro Stubbs. He must have shipped out on a long voyage, or died at sea, as sailors often did.

And then one day, when Johnny returned from an errand, he found the sailor waiting for him in the wigmaker's shop. Jethro waved a piece of paper at Johnny.

"Come along, lad," he told the boy. "I've just bought your bond-paper — so's you can tear it up! Now get your things. We're off to the Spanish Main!"

It took Johnny no time at all to pack his few belongings, heave his small bundle on his back, and follow his newfound benefactor out of the wigmaker's shop forever.

First the sailor took Johnny to Long Wharf, where he handed the boy his bond of indenture, telling him to tear it up and throw it in the sea. And Johnny did that, watching the scraps float away on the tide. He was free! Jethro Stubbs grinned, roughly brushed Johnny's tousled hair, then clapped him on the shoulder.

"Let's go, matey!" he said.

They found the recruiting officer on State Street. So urgently did the *Constitution* need a crew that Johnny soon found himself on her decks.

Johnny was not the only boy aboard. He was one of thirty sharp-tongued, irrepressible boys who skylarked about the decks because at the moment nothing was required of them. When the ship was under way, however, a thin-lipped New England schoolmaster would conduct school. They would have to struggle and sweat over sums and spelling just as if they were on land. When they were not at school, they would have to make themselves handy about the decks, scrubbing and scouring with the rest of the crew.

The *Constitution* had now signed up about four hundred officers and men. The fine uniforms of the officers were still a wonderment to Johnny, as were the gray uniforms of the natty Marines who patrolled the decks with muskets. The Marine Corps was a newly created service. While every sailor and every boy on the ship had a duty to fight as well as to work the ship, the Marines had the sole duty of fighting. Soldiers of the sea, they had no part in the work or life of the crew.

Everything about the frigate was new, fresh, spick-and-span. The copperwork glittered like the gold on the officers' uniforms. The sails, white and unstained by weather as yet, hung in graceful furls about the masts. The upper deck, or spar deck, was clean and white. The lower deck, or gun deck, had been painted a bright red. All gun decks were painted red, Johnny learned, to hide bloodstains.

There the ship's big guns, the Long Toms, were lined up on their wooden carriages, each gun facing its porthole. They could hurl a twenty-four-pound ball of solid iron the distance of a mile. But since these guns had no sights, they could be aimed in only the crudest manner. Heavy rope hawsers, attached to the barrels by rings, swung them to left or to right. A barrel could also be raised or lowered with a heavy wooden block called a quoin. Thus, these menacing black guns were not too effective at any distance.

Cannonballs were known as round shot. Grapeshot, or canister, was also used for ammunition. This was a cluster of smaller iron shot held together in a sack and used at shorter range. Ships usually fought grappled close to one another, trying to cripple each other with guns while the crews waited to board the enemy ship with cutlasses.

At such close quarters, the crude cannon could be murderous.

Up on the spar deck were also a few guns — fat, chunky little carronades. These had no range and could be used only at short distances.

It was Johnny's job to serve the No. 8 gun crew on the gun deck. At least, that was his battle station. Every sailor aboard had both a station aloft and a battle station.

The crew had worked at loading last-minute supplies and now there was little for them to do but loaf about and wait for the order to sail. It would come at any moment, the old sailors said, just as soon as the wind was right.

Some were happy at the thought of going off on a year's adventure. These whistled or sang as they traded small belongings, mended their clothes, and put things in order for the long voyage. Others looked gloomy, wishing now that they could back out at the last minute. They cursed the fate that had made them sailors, that drove them to sign on with ships again and again, even though each time they swore they would forsake the hard life of the sea and become landlubbers.

As for Johnny, he felt wildly elated. All the talk he had heard, the gossip and yarns of the old sea dogs, spun around and around in his head. The Spanish Main . . . pirate haunts . . . tropical islands of monkeys, macaws, and picaroons . . . The scraps of conversation told of a hard life, but of lots of adventure, too. The talk went on and on while the men waited for the wind to change.

It changed quite suddenly, and the order came: "Pipe all hands!"

The shrill notes of the boatswain's fife brought every man and boy up on deck, where they stood at muster while the drummer beat a roll.

The captain himself took the polished speaking trumpet and gave the next order: "All hands — up anchor!"

Amid cheers the crew scattered, each to his post. The first lieutenant now took the trumpet: "Man the bars!"

The capstan crew took their places at the capstan bars.

"Heave around!" was the next order.

The boatswain and his mate piped a merry sailors' tune, "Off She Goes!" To its notes the men at the capstan tramped around and around, muscles straining, feet beating lively time to the music, as the anchor's heavy cable coiled around the barrel-shaped piece of timber like thread on a spool.

"All hands — make sail!"

Now it was the turn of the men in the rigging. They scrambled up into the clouds like monkeys, each crew vying to be first. One after another the great white sails burst open. The masts strained like trees in a great wind. The rigging creaked as the wind caught the heavy sails.

The *Constitution* slid away from her moorings. Faster and faster went the fifer's tune. The gap of water between ship and wharf widened.

Some of the men had tears in their eyes. Some were

perched in the rigging, cheering for all they were worth. A great crowd of people had gathered on the wharf to see the ship off and wish her godspeed on her maiden voyage. They waved at the crew, their handkerchiefs, hats, scarves, and shawls making bright patterns of color in the brilliant sunshine.

The crew waved back at the wharves of Boston, the steeples, the crooked, cobbled streets. Slowly the frigate headed toward the open sea.

CHAPTER II

Off the Spanish Main

*T*WO YEARS AT SEA and Johnny was no longer under-sized, pale, and freckled. He was tough and wiry and had added as many inches to his height as he had spent years on board. His face was tanned with wind and sun. He walked with a swagger, and he seemed to have been born to the roll of a deck underfoot, the creaking of masts and flapping of sail overhead. He now felt himself a toughened man of the sea and looked with disdain on the greenhorns who stumbled about unhandily on a ship's deck. The weird moan of the rigging at night was pleasant music to him, like the chirping of crickets to a country boy.

He had been in and out of many a West Indies port as well as the South American ports of the Spanish dons. Like an old hand he could spin a tall tale about press-gangs, fistfights, and other exploits ashore. It amused

Jethro Stubbs to see how the boy imitated sailor talk and sailor swagger.

In all there were thirty "powder monkeys" aboard the man-of-war. Johnny had fought with every one of the other boys in their rough-and-tumble games and very often had taken a whipping at the gangway for his skinned knuckles. Whipping was the most frequent way of enforcing discipline on a ship. Some captains and mates were excessively cruel, believing that the more a crew was flogged, the higher its morale would be. So the common sailors stuck together. There was an unwritten law that a sailor never told on a shipmate. Often Johnny had seen a man take a whipping for another's mistake, or a whole gang whipped together because the officer could not tell which had done wrong. It was all part of a sailor's hard life.

Neither was sudden death new to Johnny by now. It happened frequently at sea. Men fell from high masts, sometimes to dash their brains out on deck, sometimes to vanish in the ocean. The mysterious "ship's fever" — probably typhus — occasionally ran through a ship, mortally infecting men overnight. This too was part of the hazardous life of a sailor.

"It's a hard life, Johnny, but show me a better," Jethro Stubbs often said.

And Johnny Griggs, though but twelve years old, feeling himself a man with a man's hard store of experience, could not even dream of a landlubber's life again. There

were times like the present, when wind and weather
were so right the crew did not have to work the ship but
could lie in the sun and watch the gulls or the porpoises.
Or nights under strange constellations, the ship spinning
a phosphorescent wake on the black water, when old
hands told tales of wonder and adventure — of haunted
ships, of plague ships, of ports far away on the other
side of the world. These were the times a sailor felt
repaid for all the hardships and dangers, when he would
not have traded places with a lord.

"Just look at our speed!" said one of the sailors ad-
miringly. "Lads, I say this is the finest frigate afloat. I'll
bet a year's grog — and you might all know, lads, how
I like my rum and ruin — that she can beat anything
that sails on any ocean tops'ls under!"

"Bah!" growled another sailor. "All we've done so far
is chase up and down these waters. But never a Frenchie
have we seen, nor yet a prize taken. Crack ship, eh?
Well, let her win a bit of glory for herself, then!"

"'Tain't the old girl's fault," the first sailor admon-
ished sharply, "if the French fleet's hiding from us, safe
in Spanish ports. Don't worry — there's glory aplenty
in store for her yet!"

"I'd like to see a little of it, then," said the disgruntled
sailor. "It's the *Constellation* that's won all the glory so
far!"

The men were silent, envying the *Constitution*'s sister
ship, built and launched in Baltimore. The *Constellation*

had already fought a glorious battle at sea and captured a French man-of-war. Her fame had traveled even through the British navy, also at war with Napoleonic France, and at every port where the *Constitution* put in, or whenever she hailed another ship at sea for news, her crew heard nothing but ecstatic praises for the Baltimore frigate.

One day a British captain came aboard. He was an old friend of Commodore Silas Talbot, the *Constitution*'s present commander, and they had drunk toasts together in many a port. The British captain said he had heard so much about this new type of Yankee frigate that he would like to look her over.

The commodore got out his crew in white muster clothes, and as the party of officers passed by the men heard the British captain say, "She's a beautifully modeled ship, sir, but damme, with these heavy guns and heavy masts she can't possibly have any speed. She's too overloaded for her own good!"

The commodore smiled and shrugged his shoulders. "Oh, as to that, we *do* carry twenty-four-pound cannon, while the most your frigates carry is eighteen."

"But that's as much as any frigate can carry and sail easily."

"We doubt that. She sails easily, for all her heavy armament."

"She certainly is an odd construction," said the British captain, looking about him with a puzzled air.

He was referring to the way the *Constitution*'s hull tapered from gun deck to spar deck. She was widest at the gun deck. From there, her lines sloped inward and upward to the spar deck. British frigates, the type that commanded the seas, were all widest at the top.

Talbot explained that the Yankee shipbuilders had thought the new design would make the *Constitution* a steadier ship, and that it would keep her from rolling under in a heavy sea. In rough weather, frigates of the English type frequently rolled so far that their gun ports were under water, a disadvantage if the guns had to be used. It was hoped that this would not happen to the *Constitution*.

"Impossible. Impossible," said the British captain, shaking his head. "I say she's too heavy for her own good and won't sail worth a farthing!"

"Why, try her, then!" cried Talbot. "She can outsail your type of wall-sided wagon any time!"

The British captain smiled. "Then let us make a sporting bet. I challenge you to a race — a day's sailing, with a cask of the finest Madeira wine as the prize. What do you say, Commodore? Have you that much confidence in your newfangled frigate?"

Talbot took the bet, and a date was set for the contest. The rival captains shook hands and parted.

For days the talk in the forecastle was of nothing but Talbot's wager with the British captain.

"Ah! Who'll get the prize, anyhow?" groused one old

sailor. "Commodore and officers will drink the Madeira, and us poor devils get maybe an extra swallow from the grog tub. That's what *we'll* win!"

"'Tain't just a barrel of wine!" cried Johnny Griggs. "It's more'n that at stake!"

"That's right," agreed another sailor. "We *think* this frigate can outsail anything in her class, but she's never been put to the test."

"Well, we'd better give a good account of ourselves," the old sailor replied. "Those British are the world's best seamen."

"And they think we're just a parcel of green bushwhackers," Johnny cried. "But we'll show 'em, won't we?"

When the men learned that the commodore had put Lieutenant Isaac Hull in command to take complete charge of the race, they went through their paces with a will. Young, impetuous, a bit rough-spoken, and by no means handsome, Hull was serving his second year aboard the *Constitution*. The men liked and respected him because he was a humane officer, and besides, he could handle the ship "better'n the Old Man himself."

Now the ship was groomed as if she were a racehorse. Everything aboard was made shipshape. Every bit of rigging was inspected and put in perfect order.

At dawn on the day of the race, when the ship's colors went up the crew did not have to be piped out of their

Activities aboard a man-of-war: repairing the ship's side; topsail-yard look-out; heaving the lead; scrubbing wash clothes. (From Heck's *Iconographic Encyclopedia*)

hammocks. Every man of them, from the smallest powder monkey to the commodore in swabs and gold cock-
ade, was already on deck.

The day had dawned fair, with a brisk breeze. One
after another the great sails shook out. The helmsman
brought the ship around until she faced into the wind.

"And now, boys," cried Hull, "we're off!"

The men cheered wildly.

"Mr. Fifer, give us a tune! And men, sing with all
your might to put heart in her!"

At the top of their lungs, the crew sang "Yankee
Doodle." From the decks of the British frigate came the
sound of bugles and of "Rule, Britannia." The men on
the *Constitution* sang louder, laughed, and burst into
cheers to drown their rivals out.

The ship headed bravely into the wind, leaning hard
on her side, sliding briskly and easily through the water.
The British ship was moving too, gathering speed as it
went.

The race was to windward — that is, both ships were
to sail with wind and sea dead ahead. A ship can sail
against the wind only by tacking, taking a zigzag course
to its destination and cutting into the wind at a sharp
angle, with the wind first on one side of the ship and
then on the other. Too sharp an angle makes a ship slow
down, or make leeway. Too wide an angle forces a ship
to make longer and longer tacks, thus traveling farther

to its destination. It takes fine seamanship and thorough knowledge of a ship's behavior to get the most out of it in such maneuvers.

Isaac Hull knew his ship. He kept the angle with the wind neither too sharp nor too wide.

All day long the frigate forged into the heavy spray, all hands on duty. During some tacks the men rushed to the windward side to keep the frigate as nearly upright as possible so that she might hold a better wind. When the helmsman brought the ship's head around for the next tack and the wind spilled out and the sails were aflutter, Hull knew how to ease her so as not to lose a moment of time. Then, as the sails filled out again on the other side, the crew rushed to the opposite rail, hoarsely cheering and tumbling over one another to help the ship get headway again.

With each skillful tack the Yankee frigate drew further and further ahead of her competitor.

"Tops'ls under it'll be!" Hull cried. "We've won, men, we've won!"

The British frigate was indeed left so far behind that when the sunset gun sounded, her topsails had dipped below the horizon. Only the white flash of her topgallants and royals were visible in the rays of the setting sun.

So Isaac Hull proved the worth of the new navy and won the commodore his cask of Madeira. The British captain and his officers brought the prize aboard.

"To the Yankee frigates!" the captain toasted gallantly. "May we never run foul of 'em at sea!"

Long into the night the crew made merry. Extra grog had been served, and there was dancing in the forecastle and games on deck. No officers harried the men for relaxed discipline, for they too were celebrating, clinking glasses with the British officers and sharing the commodore's prize cask.

The shadow war with Napoleonic France was drawing to a close. It had never been much of a war anyway. Of the three frigates built for the new little navy — the *United States*, the *Constellation*, and the *Constitution* — only the *Constellation* had gathered glory. News came that she had again defeated a French ship, *La Vengeance*, in a furious battle off Guadeloupe. The British papers were hysterical with praise. Gifts from London poured in on the *Constellation*'s captain.

But there was no such luck for the *Constitution*. Her days of glory were still to come, in other wars.

In fact, a war in earnest now seemed to be brewing with those Mediterranean pirates in North Africa.

CHAPTER III

To the Shores of Tripoli

HE BARBARY COAST was named for a famous North
*T*African pirate, Barbarossa, whose name meant "red
beard." He and his cohorts had preyed upon Mediterranean shipping in the sixteenth century so fiercely and
cruelly, and apparently with such success in amassing
wealth in this way, that piracy was still practiced officially by the states of North Africa well into modern
times. These states were ruled by three corsair kings:
the dey of Algiers, the bey of Tunis, and the bashaw of
Tripoli. These pirate kings had grown increasingly arrogant toward the young United States in their demands
for tribute. The countries of Europe regularly sent them
such blackmail money to protect their ships. But the
corsair kings kept demanding larger and larger sums and
the American people were grumbling. Failing to get
more tribute, they threatened war. Even Congress at last
grew tired of appeasing these ruffians.

After two squadrons had returned without accomplishing anything, a third was organized to sail and crack down in earnest on the robber kings. The *Constitution* was the flagship of this squadron.

In 1803 she was once again signing on a crew. But now her sailors had changed. No longer mostly New Englanders, her men and boys came from almost every state and reflected all the colorful immigrant strains of the fast-growing country. Besides native Yankees there were Germans from Philadelphia, Irish from New York, Danes, Dutch, Portuguese, and even a Hindustani, a barber. Freeborn Negroes from the North enlisted as galley cooks, and one or two joined the foretop crew and gun crew.

Among the recruits was a young seaman, tanned and wiry, with a small scar along one cheek; he was a stripling of sixteen or thereabouts, just barely of age to be signed on at full seaman's pay. He looked keenly disappointed when told that the *Constitution* already had her full gun crew, and that his shipmate, a crack gunner, would therefore not be able to sign on with him. But there was room for Jethro Stubbs aboard the schooner *Nautilus*, another ship of the squadron. He and Johnny, now called Jack, Griggs would meet again at their destination, even if they would not be messmates for the coming two years.

"See you in Africa!" the red-bearded sailor yelled as they parted. "You're on your own now, Jack my lad — so keep your weather eye alifting!"

Thus, after a stretch in the merchant service, Seaman Jack Griggs was once again on the decks of the *Constitution*. She had been his first ship. He felt real affection for her gallant lines and stout masts. And he was lucky to get a berth aboard her just in time, for now she was really sailing to Africa, the lair of the pirate kings.

The squadron consisted of seven ships. Like the flagship, the frigate *Philadelphia* carried forty-four guns. The rest were vessels of lighter draft and armament: the sixteen–gun brigs *Argus* and *Siren*, and the schooners *Vixen* and *Nautilus* carrying fourteen and twelve guns. Another twelve–gun schooner, the *Enterprise*, under command of Stephen Decatur, was already stationed in the Mediterranean waiting to join them.

"We're lucky not to be aboard the *Philadelphia*," an old salt told the young seaman. "That there ship's jinxed!"

"How so?"

"It's her cap'n. Name's Bainbridge. Bad luck follers him everywhere. You wait an' see — he'll run her into trouble."

"Not that it's primroses here, either," another sailor put in. "The commodore's a hell-buster. Got the men walkin' backwards on their tippy-toes to keep out of his way, and the officers all fallin' over each other. His eyes look marlinespikes and he spits gunpowder. Yestiddy he bawled out the captain himself, and you could hear him clear across to Africa."

It was true that Commodore Edward Preble's choleric temper was feared by officers and crew alike. The Old Man had come up the hard way, "through the hawse-hole," as the men described an officer who had worked his way up from the ranks. Fifteen years he had knocked about the sea, and his disposition was permanently pick-led by salt water. In one of his vile tempers he was capable of bawling out the angel Gabriel himself in front of the lowest-ranking, grinning little powder monkey aboard. His staff of officers, young lieutenants to a man, came in for a heavy share of his sarcasm.

Who, he wondered, had ever heard of these schoolboys — Stephen Decatur, Dick Somers, Isaac Hull, and the rest? How could he trust his precious ships to them? Fight a war with them? Any way you looked at it, he had seven ships and a thousand men against twenty-five thousand Tripolitans with twenty-four ships and a shore battery of a hundred and nineteen guns. Instead of being given men of resourcefulness and experience to help him in this difficult and dangerous task, he had these young mollycoddles to command his ships!

One by one, the ships of the squadron sailed: the *Argus*, with Isaac Hull in command; the *Siren*, under Charles Stewart; the schooners *Nautilus* and *Vixen*, in charge of Dick Somers and John Smith. And, thought the Old Man sourly, not a full-grown man in the lot. You'd think he was running a school for cubs instead of a bloody war.

At Gibraltar Preble learned he had still another war on his hands. The emperor of Morocco had just declared war on the United States! One of his pirate ships, the *Mirboka*, had captured a Boston brig and taken all her crew prisoners. But Bainbridge in the *Philadelphia* had met up with the *Mirboka* and captured her in turn. The emperor wanted his ship back. He called the retaliation an act of war. So Preble went off to Morocco in the *Constitution* to see whether the sight of a few guns might persuade the emperor to change his mind.

He left the captured *Mirboka* at Gibraltar for safe-keeping, with some of his crew aboard. And there, in Preble's absence, something happened that showed how America was drawing closer and closer to war with a great sea power — England.

Three Yankee sailors stationed aboard the *Mirboka* deserted. They made their way to town and disappeared. Two young officers, Midshipman Charles Morris from the *Constitution* and Midshipman McDonough from the *Philadelphia*, were sent to arrest them and bring them back to the ship.

Since Gibraltar was a British naval base, Morris and McDonough thought the likeliest place to look would be outside the British dockyard, for there the deserters would probably try to get a berth aboard a British ship. Sure enough, they caught sight of the three deserters sauntering along toward the British sentry. Both officers called the men by name and ran after them.

The sailors were big, ruffianly fellows, in contrast to the smooth-faced young officers. The sight of their pursuers, however, threw the three into a panic. They scattered, each man fleeing in a different direction.

Morris and McDonough each got one prisoner, but the third deserter escaped by running past the British sentry into the dockyard. The two Yankee officers begged a favor of the sentry. Would he take charge of their two prisoners for them while they went inside to get the third man?

They were a little surprised at the way the sentry so readily agreed to help them. As they passed inside the dockyard, McDonough muttered to his companion, "D'you think he mistook us for British officers?"

Then they caught sight of the third man, Evans. He was escaping in a rowboat, heading for a British frigate at anchor out in the harbor. The two midshipmen ran toward the beach, shouting to the fugitive to put back. This made the deserter row faster toward the British ship.

"You're under arrest!" Morris cried. "Come back or we'll go after you!"

"You've no rights over me!" the deserter called back. "You'll not put Bill Evans in irons! I'm a Britisher, that's what!"

McDonough swore. "You're a disgrace to your country! You won't get away with this, Evans!"

"You keep your hands off me," Evans called back, "or you'll get into trouble!"

"Dirty, renegade polecat," McDonough muttered furiously.

He and Morris watched their man climb aboard the British ship.

"Come!" Morris said. "Let's get a boat. We're going after him!"

They rowed out to the frigate and went aboard. When they asked to see the captain, they were told to wait. The hot Mediterranean sun beat down on the deck. No one troubled to show the two visitors any small courtesy or even to offer them a place to sit down. An hour passed, and another. The crew went casually about their work, elaborately ignoring the two Americans.

"They're hiding our prisoner and laughing up their sleeves while we fry here," McDonough muttered angrily.

"I swear we'll not move from here," Morris said furiously, "until we see that captain face to face, blast him!"

McDonough wiped his perspiring forehead and went over to one of the British sailors who was loafing on deck. He asked for a glass of water.

The sailor shrugged and carelessly turned his back.

"Scuttlebutt's nearby," he said indifferently, meaning that the scuttlebutt, or water cask, was good enough for American officers.

Morris and McDonough both turned red. They looked at one another, scowling but helpless. The entire ship seemed to be in on the conspiracy.

"Well, I've been frying here long enough," said McDonough. "I'm going to drink anyway at their filthy scuttlebutt."

He went for his drink, but it had little cooling effect on his mounting temper. "They're all laughing at us," he growled. "Ah, but I'd like to make 'em laugh out of the other side of their faces!"

At length the British captain sent for them.

Morris spoke up, choking back his anger as best he could. "Sir, there's an American seaman named Bill Evans aboard your ship. He's a deserter from the United States frigate *Constitution* and is under arrest. We've come to take him back to be disciplined."

The British captain smiled unpleasantly. "Can you prove your man an American? He claims to be British. As such, I intend to protect him."

"He's lying, then!" McDonough exploded.

The British captain shrugged. His manner became frosty. "Since you can't prove anything, I intend to keep him. And any others like him! This man claims you have many other British aboard your frigate and that you are keeping them there by force. We shall take steps to make you give them up!"

Pale with fury, Morris told the captain, "There are no British aboard, and you know it!"

"We've taken men off your ships before," said the captain, "and we'll do it again if we choose to."

"You'll not do it again!" said Morris, trembling, his voice rising and choking. The British captain laughed. Morris managed to get his voice steady enough to deliver a final ultimatum: "For the last time, sir, I make formal demand for this man, an American deserter. I insist that you give him up to me!"

But the captain refused to surrender their man, and coolly dismissed them.

Infuriated but helpless, the two young officers returned to shore to pick up their other two prisoners. There the sentry, pretending innocence, claimed to know nothing about any prisoners. So now they had lost all three men, and there was nothing for it but to go back to their ship empty-handed.

Meanwhile, simply by sailing into Tangier with four ships, the commodore had persuaded the emperor of Morocco, known to his subjects as "the Abode of Happiness," to conclude peace with the United States. Preble won back the captive Yankee sailors without payment of any tribute and, that little bit of business disposed of, ordered the *Mirboka* returned to the emperor.

The report of what had happened in his absence threw Preble into one of his terrible rages. McDonough, who was now back aboard the *Philadelphia*, escaped the storm, which fell with full effect on the unlucky Morris. When the quivering young midshipman recounted how the British captain had threatened to come aboard the *Constitution* to look for Britishers, Preble's howls were heard all over the ship. The men nudged one another. Old Sourpuss was letting one of his "schoolboys" have it again.

"Do you know we're not at war with England?" Preble bellowed. 'D'you know that, mister? We've trouble enough on our hands without every popinjay in a monkey suit provoking incidents with the British!"

"But, sir!" Morris protested, shocked. "Our prisoner was aboard. It was our *duty* to bring him back!"

"What about the other prisoners?" Preble roared. "Weren't two good enough for you?"

"They got away, sir. The British guard released them."

"Oh, he did, eh? What did you expect him to do? Escort them to the *Mirboka* for you? Idiot! Fool! Nincompoop! Get out of my sight so I can figure out what to do with you!"

The young man felt his disgrace keenly. There was no corner of the ship where he could be alone. Who hadn't heard the Old Man tell him off?

His messmate and friend, Henry Wadsworth, came

over and pressed his hand. "Don't feel so low, Charlie. I don't think it's you the Old Man is really angry at, but that British captain."

"I suppose," said Morris bitterly, "I'll be put under arrest for doing my duty!"

Even Wadsworth was expecting nothing short of arrest and disgrace for his friend. Preble went about the deck of the *Constitution* with the icy look of a codfish, treating all his officers as if they were beneath his notice.

Much later, Wadsworth came over to his messmate with a dazed look on his face. "Charles! I just overheard the Old Man telling the lieutenant he'd finally made up his mind what to do with you."

"Ordered my arrest, I suppose."

"No. Not that. Not that at all! He said you'd be in irons, all right, if it weren't for the way you sassed that British captain. For that, he's going to give you a special, responsible assignment. Now what do you think of that? He actually had a smile on his face — it looked as if an earthquake had shifted all his features. You know, I sometimes think the old swab's almost human!"

CHAPTER IV

Yankee Schoolboys

*T*HE SHIPS of the squadron were on their way to Malta when the *Constitution* hailed a British ship. The friendly British captain came aboard for a nip and a chat in Preble's cabin. He was the bearer of disastrous news.

The pirates of Tripoli had captured the *Philadelphia*, with all her crew!

The news stunned Preble. How had it happened? The fo'c'sle gossip seemed to be right — Bainbridge was walking misfortune. There were three hundred men aboard the *Philadelphia*, a third of Preble's manpower. And with the loss of the squadron's only other frigate, Preble's offensive power had been cut virtually in two.

"How many hurt, or killed?" Preble asked next. The Barbary corsairs were savage, but usually preferred to take prisoners because they could get ransom for them.

"Oh, not a man!" the captain assured Preble.

"They're all safe. That is, Captain Bainbridge and his officers are in the pirates' filthy prison, and as for the crew, they're being sold as slaves."

For days after this, instead of flying off the handle at every small mishap, Preble kept to his cabin and brooded silently with his head in his hands. Now he had to fight a war with only one frigate, because Bainbridge had lost him his second.

At Malta, letters came from Bainbridge in prison. He explained how the *Philadelphia* had fallen into such hard luck. She had been trying to maintain a blockade of Tripoli harbor when a corsair attempted to make a run for it. The pursuing frigate was trickily led onto a shoal, where she grounded. With her bottom stove in, the *Philadelphia* was helpless when the bashaw's gunboats came flocking around her like hawks to a feast. There was nothing Bainbridge could do but surrender. There was no way to get his men ashore. It was no use having his men killed or maimed to no purpose. Thus 307 Yankee men and officers were disastrously delivered into slavery.

The bashaw, pleased with his fine bit of Yankee shipbuilding, had given orders to plug up the *Philadelphia*'s holes and float her. He considered her a welcome addition to his pirate fleet.

All of Preble's young officers seethed with indignation. They talked of nothing else but how the *Philadelphia* might be avenged.

"I'd rather see her at the bottom of the sea," Decatur said bitterly, "than in such dishonorable service!"

"Or to see her turning her guns on the *Constitution!*" cried Dick Somers.

"Let's take the whole squadron there — what's left of it," said the impetuous Hull, "and if we can't recapture the *Philadelphia*, we'll blow her to bits with our guns!"

The Old Man smiled coldly and pointed out that the *Philadelphia* was much too well guarded. Even if they could get into the harbor, it was almost certain that they would not get out again.

Tripoli was a walled city, well fortified. Two headlands crowned with grim gray forts guarded the mouth of the harbor. There was a mole, or breakwater, beside which ships had to sail in. The mole, too, had a powerful array of batteries. Two miles of treacherous shoals provided a further, natural protection.

Inside the harbor the bashaw's own gunboats swarmed. Behind the city walls, over which floated the flag of piracy, were more frowning bastions. Even the bashaw's palace, and his Maltese castle, showed a row of guns like black teeth against the sky. The town was so heavily fortified that it looked like a city of prisons.

The Old Man could not risk his ships. But he was hatching a plan of his own, a daring deed that, if successful, would cheer his men and lift their sinking morale. For, with the Bainbridge disaster, a great many felt the war as good as lost already.

Preble was weighing his "schoolboy" officers, going over each one in his mind, trying to decide which would be the most trustworthy and daring to carry out his plan.

There was Stephen Decatur, barely entering his twenties — hawk-nosed, crisp- and curly-haired, keen-eyed. Talked back, too, when it suited him. The Old Man had a growing and healthy respect for this youngster.

And there was pleasant Dick Somers. You'd think him mild as milk, only in a pinch he would show himself brave as any, steady and cool.

Young Isaac Hull, now, had had some experience in that affair of the *Sandwich*. He had stolen into a West Indies port in broad daylight, captured a French corvette, the *Sandwich*, spiked the three shore cannon guarding her, and then made off with his rich prize without bloodshed. A man of action, a bit impetuous and hotheaded. Somewhat like the Old Man himself . . .

Well, it was true, Preble thought, they were all just boys. But they were *good* boys. They craved some action. It was time they had it.

"Boys," Preble told them, "we are not going to try anything so foolhardy as force. We are not going to risk the loss of the *Constitution* or of a single gunboat. Nevertheless, we are going to go in there and burn the *Philadelphia*, send her to the bottom of the bay where she'll lie until kingdom come, and where no foreign power'll ever have the use of her!"

The plan was to fool the Tripolitans by posing as

Maltese traders. The squadron had recently captured a small pirate ketch with a lateen rig, the *Mastico*, put a Yankee crew aboard her, and renamed her the *Intrepid*. Her triangular sail, the kind used by all the Barbary Coast vessels, would arouse no suspicion. The Americans could use the ketch to slip into the harbor and undertake the hazardous job of firing the *Philadelphia*.

As Preble outlined his plan, his men's eyes lit eagerly. Together they worked out all the details. Armed men — the pick of the squadron, as many as could be packed in — would be hidden in the hold. Only a few would be allowed up for air at a time, and those on deck would be dressed like Maltese. The ketch would undertake her perilous mission at night, to give her the best chance to sneak in — and, if possible in the confusion, to get out again as best she could.

For the tricky harbor they needed a pilot who knew the lay of the land thoroughly, preferably one who could speak Maltese and do all the talking with the Tripolitans. They had such a man, the *Mastico*'s former pilot, who professed to be willing to work for the Yankees. Upon him the entire success or failure of the plan actually depended.

It was young Stephen Decatur whom Preble chose to take command of the ketch. The others, of course, all envied him. This was their first chance to prove their worth against the arrogant corsairs.

Decatur carefully picked his crew from among those

who volunteered — about sixty men, the bravest and the most dependable. In addition he selected three lieutenants and six midshipmen. Decatur's crew was almost complete when a very young seaman tugged at his sleeve, respectfully touched his cap, and begged to be taken along.

"Why do you want to go along, Jack?" asked Decatur, amused.

"Well, sir, you see, I'd kinder like to see the country."

He grinned so engagingly that Decatur hadn't the heart to refuse, even though he had picked the most sea-hardened tars for this dangerous mission.

"All right, Jack. Come along. But you take the place of a full-grown man, understand? A man's work and a man's fighting!"

"I am a man, sir," said Jack Griggs seriously.

Preparations were now quickly made. The *Intrepid* made a trip to Syracuse and loaded up with gunpowder, tar, pitch, oakum, and turpentine.

It was decided that the ketch would not go alone, after all, but would be accompanied by the *Siren*. The *Siren* would hover close by under cover of darkness, and her boats would be waiting to pick up the crew if the *Intrepid* met with some serious accident.

The order to sail came so suddenly that there was no time to prepare stores. On February 3, 1804, the ketch was under way after one hour's notice.

Completely dependent as the *Intrepid* was on weather,

when she started out no man of her crew could guess how long she would be gone. At that time of the year especially there were wild storms off North Africa. The dreaded levanter, a howling east wind, could blow for days and pile ships upon the rocky shore. In such weather a ship simply rode out the fury of the storm under bare poles, with deadlights in and portholes closed. She tried to keep far from shore and was often blown far off course.

The ketch had quarters for about a dozen men. There were close to seventy aboard. To make things worse, she carried short supplies. After the first day out the men found that the food was spoiled. They had nothing to eat but bread and water.

In about a week they reached Tripoli.

Out of sight of other vessels for the moment, the men crowded at the rail. The officers passed the spyglass to one another, pointing out the landmarks — the famous forts, the bashaw's castle, the prison where at this very minute Captain Bainbridge was confined. As they slipped nearer they could see the rooftops of the town and the mosques and minarets behind the city's white walls.

Some of the men shook their fists. There in the town, Yankee bluejackets from the *Philadelphia* were being put up for sale in the slave marts. Bearded Mussulmen in long robes would look them over, pinch them to see how strong their muscles were, bid for them, and take them away in chains. Heavy iron collars would be locked about their necks. Many would not survive until ransom came from home.

The harbor was crowded with all the colorful vessels of the Mediterranean, some dating from the most ancient times — Spanish xebecs, Moorish feluccas, Arab dhows, Turkish galleys. These last, vessels without sails, were propelled by human labor: Christian captives were chained to the long oars, or sweeps, and beaten by overseers. Such a fate might even be in store for some of the crew of the *Philadelphia*.

Everywhere, like watchful hawks, hovered the bashaw's own fleet of modern gunboats. A stiff wind was blowing up. The sea was rough, the sky low and sullen. Lines of white froth showed a heavy surf pounding the shore.

By nightfall the little ketch had slid up near the harbor entrance and dropped anchor. The wind increased steadily in pitch, wailing eerily in the rigging. The darkness was black and absolute. Not a star glimmered in the heavily blanketed sky.

The men were all on deck, keyed up, waiting for Decatur to give the order.

Salvatore Catalano, the Maltese pilot, shrugged his heavy shoulders. "Bad," he said. He added in Sicilian, "Devil's weather! No good!"

"I'll tell you what, sir," said Midshipman Morris to

the captain. "Let me go out with the pilot in a small boat and see how the surf is running at the harbor entrance. Then we'll see if we can chance it."

The boat returned. Catalano climbed out in dripping oilskins, followed by the young midshipman. Both shook their heads.

"It's impossible," Morris said. "We'll have to turn back!"

"It's cowardice to turn back now!" one of the officers cried angrily.

Morris flushed, but held firm. "We'd only run aground then, and meet the same fate as the *Philadelphia*."

Still Decatur hesitated.

"We'll let the pilot decide!"

But Catalano shook his head vigorously.

This put a damper on the rest. Reluctantly Decatur gave the order to put about.

By daylight the sea was boiling like a pot. A howling gale hurled both the *Intrepid* and the *Siren* farther and farther asea. They tried to keep in sight of one another, but this soon became impossible. The ketch strained and tossed, scudding along under bare poles, spars pitching almost horizontally. Though it was winter, peals of thunder could be heard. Lightning lit a wild, stormy scene. The crew, most of them believers in the supernatural, worried that the storm might be a bad omen, a sign that their luck would not continue.

Down in the hold, they slept on the same barrels that held their water supply. The round staves almost broke their backs as the ship pitched and tossed. They became covered with sores and bruises. The hold was smelly, stuffy, frightfully overcrowded. Many were seasick. To make it worse, the pirates had left them an unwelcome legacy: the ketch was louse-ridden.

Day or night, it was much the same. The infernal gloom was only a little less thick by day. One moment of great danger occurred during one night, however. Dark shapes suddenly appeared out of the water, surrounding the vessel like a herd of seals. They were rocks. The ship had been blown too close to the treacherous coast.

The pilot, Salvatore Catalano, got them out of the rocks safely. Afterward he managed to guide the ship with only a storm staysail into a sheltered cove where she could sit tight and ride out the remainder of the storm.

"Well, I dunno," grudgingly remarked one old sailor, "but that there Eyetalian or whatever he is kin handle a ship 'most as good as any Yankee sailing master *I* ever did see!"

In the eyes of the crew, there could be no higher praise for Catalano's expert seamanship.

The gale blew on and on for five days. At last the sun rose on a calm and glittering sea. Pale, shaky, battered, the *Intrepid*'s crew headed back toward Africa. On the way they picked up the *Siren*. The two ships sighted the harbor of Tripoli on the morning of the sixteenth.

All sorts of ships that had been stormbound as they had been were now busily making port. Sailors' songs in many languages floated across the water. Salvatore Catalano sang too, a Sicilian song, waving and bellowing greetings at passing vessels.

Once again the crew was crammed below in the verminous hold. The officers kept off the deck; not a uniform showed. The dozen sailors permitted above deck wore exotic sashes, turbans, boleros, and silken trousers.

The winds were so light — just playful cat's-paws slapping the sail — that the little ketch had trouble reaching port. That must have been how it seemed to someone watching from shore. Actually Decatur was using every kind of drag — buckets, grapnels, anything that would hold the ship back until nightfall. Sure enough, the ketch managed to make the mouth of the harbor just as darkness fell.

CHAPTER V

Viking's Death of the "Philadelphia"

*T*HE YOUNG MOON hung in a thin crescent over the Moorish town. The water was still, a black mirror reflecting the yellow horn lanterns of ships riding at anchor. The wind was dying. There was scarcely enough to fill the lateen sail.

Now the crucial moment had come. Decatur and his officers were huddled around the binnacle light, coaching the pilot in the part he was to play. Everything depended on how well Catalano understood his orders and obeyed them.

A man leaning over the rail beside Jack Griggs rubbed his bruised back gingerly, scratched himself, and cursed the fattened lice that had feasted on them down in the hold. "You think we kin trust that varmint?" he whispered, nodding toward the pilot, who kept smiling broadly at everything Decatur was saying.

"He seems mighty anxious to please," Jack answered.

"I dunno," the sailor went on. "It might be he's leading us into some trap."

It was possible. The whole harbor was a trap, really. Supposing there was just the smallest hitch somewhere in their carefully rehearsed plan . . . There was enough gunpowder aboard to blow them all to kingdom come.

Jack cleared his throat and said, "A ship feels naked-like without cannon to defend itself."

"Wind's dying," growled his companion. "What in thunderation's keeping us here? Do they want us to get stranded?"

Decatur was waiting for the *Siren*'s small boats to show up. But with the wind dropping off so fast, he decided to go in alone. True, this increased their risk, but as he said, shrugging off objections, "Well, then — the fewer the number, the greater the honor!"

Quickly the officers and midshipmen went among the crew and held a rehearsal. The plan was for each officer to take a few men to a certain part of the *Philadelphia* and wait for orders to set fire.

Jack Griggs was given his station: the *Philadelphia*'s cockpit, below decks. There, if they succeeded in capturing the frigate, he and three burly tars were to take some oakum, pitch, dynamite, and other combustibles to Midshipman Charles Morris. Jack nodded soberly. Over and over he tried to rehearse in his mind everything that he must do, every single act from the moment he would set foot aboard the *Philadelphia*.

In breathless silence, the ketch slid into Tripoli harbor.

Now all her crew were ready on deck. Darkness hid them, lying side by side, officers and men alike, touching one another, conscious of each other's breathing. Under his jacket Jack Griggs fingered the sharp edge of his boarding knife. The blade was long and keen.

There was no doubt that the pilot, Catalano, knew every inch of the tricky harbor. They slid under great batteries, black and forbidding, and passed without challenge.

When he lifted his head, Jack could see the *Philadelphia*. She towered above a score or so of smaller ships anchored around her. She rose above them like a queen, and with a pang of pity Jack thought that though they had come to burn her, she would be glad to see them. And yes, she was well guarded. The white walls of a fort loomed just behind her.

Catalano was taking them straight toward the *Philadelphia* and the second set of deadly batteries. All seemed quiet on her deck. They were not suspected. But the corsairs had posted a sentry aboard the captured frigate. Suddenly a sharp challenge rang out.

Now the moment had come for Salvatore Catalano to play his crucial part. There followed a lively exchange between the pilot of the ketch and the sentry. Catalano had been instructed to say that they were Maltese traders and had lost their anchor in the storm. He was to beg for permission to tie up to the *Philadelphia* for the night.

The sentry ordered that lights be brought. Suspiciously the Tripolitans lowered lanterns and looked long and earnestly at the ketch. Not a man aboard the *Intrepid* stirred even a finger. It seemed to Jack Griggs that they had all stopped breathing.

At that very moment the wind died and the ketch swung abeam, helpless under the frigate's big guns. Under his breath Catalano swore a big, black Sicilian oath. But he laughed aloud and joked with the sentry, keeping up his steady flow of chatter.

Apparently the pirates had seen nothing suspicious after all. Gruffly they told Catalano he might tie up for the night, but warned him not to come any closer.

Decatur quickly passed the whispered word to make fast.

A rope from the *Philadelphia* was tied to a rope from the ketch. Quietly in the darkness, still lying on the deck, Decatur's men hauled the rope in hand over hand. With scarcely the sound of a ripple the ketch sneaked closer and closer to the towering frigate.

The *Philadelphia* loomed over their heads when a furious bellow aboard her threw everything into a nightmare din: "*Americanos!*"

Decatur jumped to his feet and rushed to the rail, crying as he ran, "Board her, boys!"

The whole crew swarmed behind him as one man.

On the deck of the frigate, strange shadow-shapes

rushed past in the dim light — corsairs in flowing garments and turbans, Yankees in boarding caps made of fur, like the heads of strange animals. In that dim light it was hard to tell friend from foe. Feet thudded, steel clashed against steel, hoarse cries in Arabic mingled with hearty Yankee curses.

Jack ran where everyone else seemed to be running. All his carefully rehearsed plans were forgotten. Small and agile, he made a poor target for slashing knives and yataghans, the short sabers used by the Moors. Besides, the enemy now seemed to be on the run. The Tripolitans were fleeing to the opposite rail of the *Philadelphia* and leaping into the sea.

Here and there some turned to fight, cornered and desperate. Once a turbaned pirate made a furious slash at Jack with a long, curving knife. Jack ducked, lunged at the Moor, and must have done some damage because the bearded corsair dropped his weapon and doubled over, grunting. But there was no time to wait and see. The rush and din carried Jack along.

Just ahead, a figure crouching behind a huge coil of rope sprang at an officer — at Decatur himself!

"Look out, sir!" Jack yelled.

He hurled himself at the assassin just as Decatur whirled about. Jack's light weight could not tumble the Moor over, but he did manage to deflect his aim.

As Decatur closed in with his sword, the furious Mussulman — a powerful, black-bearded giant of a man —

swung down again with his razor-sharp scimitar, making a lunge at Decatur's head. In a flash a huge, raw-boned Yankee sailor named Reuben James ducked between the two. Roughly he hurled Decatur aside, taking the full impact of the weapon on his own grizzled skull. At that very instant Jack Griggs, panting and clinging like a burr to the assassin, managed to drive his boarding knife into the corsair's back. There was a gurgling cry of pain. Decatur scrambled to his feet, unhurt.

Maddened by his wound, seemingly insensible to anything but the thought of revenge, the giant Moor lurched after Jack Griggs, swinging his scimitar wildly and without aim. Decatur would have dispatched the wounded pirate, but the black-bearded Tripolitan suddenly staggered, turned pale, and let his weapon fall to the deck. With a superhuman burst of strength he turned and disappeared in the general din and confusion.

"Well done, lad!" Decatur gasped, seizing Jack by the hand. He turned to the big sailor who stood by, grinning and still dazedly rubbing his injured skull. "You're hurt!"

"No, sir. Not a mite. You see, sir, my skull's a lot thicker'n yourn!"

Decatur laughed and wrung the sailor's hand. "You saved my life! Ask me anything you like, and it's yours!"

"I'll think on it, sir," said the sailor. And off he went after the few remaining pirates.

Now a strapping, half-naked Yankee sailor with a wild

look in his eyes ran past yelling, "Clear the decks! We've won, boys, we've won!"

He picked up a howling corsair bodily, held him in midair, and shook him. Over the rail he hurled him. With a terrific splash the Moor hit the sea.

"We've got 'em on the run, boys! Plopping into the sea like porpoises! Huzza! Huzza!"

It was true. Hardly a pirate remained aboard. Splash after splash told of the last few escaping or being tossed overboard by the exuberant Yankees. It had been easy, after all — easier than they had hoped. The fight had actually lasted only a few minutes.

They hastily cleared the decks of the dead and the dying. Miraculously, not a single Yankee had been lost. The Tripolitans had been too surprised to put up much of a fight. They had fled in panic, thinking that they were surrounded by fleets of bloodthirsty Yankees.

But by now the entire harbor was in a state of high alarm. The cry had quickly gone from ship to ship: "*Americanos! Americanos!*"

One of the bashaw's gunboats was trying to get the range of the *Philadelphia*. But the shot apparently went into one of the vessels nearby. Howls, staccato cries, and curses followed. The gunboat stopped firing — the bashaw was shooting up his own fleet.

And now the Yankee sailors worked like demons. Everything depended on timing — and on luck. They rushed the combustibles aboard. Flames were started on the upper deck. When the ship blazed, they would instantly become the target of the whole harbor.

Jack Griggs scrambled down the forward hatchway into the cockpit with his gunpowder and oakum, the three men with him carrying barrels of pitch and oil. Midshipman Morris was already there, waiting. They could hear the flames hissing and crackling above on the spar deck as they worked frantically, spreading the oil and pitch. Thick, black, and greasy smoke flooded the gun deck through the open hatchways.

"We'll be trapped below here, men!" Morris cried. "Look alive!"

While they were firing the cockpit, a section of spar deck collapsed aft, spilling flame close to a big cache of gunpowder. They fled, coughing and choking, groping their way aloft through the dense smoke of the forward hatchway.

Suddenly they were in the open, in a blaze of hellish light. They seemed to be the last men aboard the frigate. Flames were crawling at the base of her tall masts. Little rivulets of fire spread along the deck planks. The whole aft section was a spreading inferno.

They found the ketch still grappled fast to the *Philadelphia*, even though flames were pouring over from the doomed frigate, endangering the *Intrepid*. As they tumbled gasping into the ketch, Midshipman Morris cried, "Shove off, lads, for the love of God, or we'll be afire! Why don't you shove off?"

"Lieutenant Decatur's still aboard, sir." A sailor panted rapidly, squinting at the terrible heat of the flames.

At that moment Decatur appeared, brilliantly outlined against the background of fire. He leaped the flaming gap, the last to leap overboard.

The ketch was in such great danger now that the men shoved off even before he leaped. They bent every effort to getting clear of the *Philadelphia*. Her stately masts were all ablaze, like giant torches, and there was danger of their falling.

Happy as children at a bonfire, the men cheered hoarsely. One yelled, shaking his fist at the bashaw's castle, "How d'you like our Fourth o' July, ye bloody tyrant?"

As if in answer from the castle, the bashaw's guns thundered out angrily.

All the ships moored nearby had frantically moved away. Against the vivid flames, the escaping ketch was now a target for all the big guns. One hundred cannon fired away at her! The pilot, Catalano, tried to maneuver out of their range, but the winds were fitful and the men had to work hard at pulling the ketch along with sweeps.

One cannonball crashed into the topgallant sail and splintered the top of the mast. Sweating and cursing as they worked the sweeps, the men looked aloft and grinned at each other. The Tripolitans were rotten gunners!

Now there was a new danger. The *Philadelphia*'s own guns began shooting at them! Loaded by the pirates, they began exploding in the intense heat, one by one hurling grapeshot and cannonballs wildly in every direction.

Officers and men all worked frantically together, crying out at the weird beauty cast over the harbor by the dying ship. A mast fell. Fountains of spray shot into the air. Sparks whirled like burning butterflies and mingled with the spray.

The bashaw's gunboats moved in to cut off their escape. But this brought the gunboats in range of the exploding guns on the *Philadelphia* and forced them to move back again — and the passage was left clear. At that, the wildest cheering of all broke out aboard the ketch.

"She's standing by us!" a man yelled.

"She's seeing us through!"

"Huzza for the *Philadelphia!*"

"God bless her! Huzza! Huzza!"

It was as though ghostly gunners on the pyre of the frigate's decks manned those guns to cover the ketch's escape from the harbor. And then, providentially, a light breeze sprang up. Catalano guided the Americans skillfully past blazing forts and the grim, dark headlands to the harbor entrance, where darkness sheltered them.

Sometime during those tense moments when the small, undefended ketch was running the gauntlet of all the guns in the harbor, the *Philadelphia*'s magazine caught fire. In a terrific explosion of rockets and glory, she went to her Viking's death.

The great light was blotted from the harbor.

Castles, forts, flamelit masts, and rigging all magically vanished.

The guns were suddenly still.

CHAPTER VI

Battle of Tripoli Bay

"SALVATORE CATALANO — *Americano!*"

The pilot of the victorious ketch flashed his strong white teeth in an amiable smile and thumped his sturdy chest. He had blossomed out in the natty uniform of a Yankee bluejacket: a glossy hat with dangling ribbons; a short, tight blue coat; and wide white petticoat trousers. As one of the chief heroes of the expedition, he came in for a big share of the glory and congratulations.

He wanted to go to America and become a Yankee sailing master, and all the men agreed there was nothing Catalano couldn't sail. He had been amply rewarded for his share in the expedition, and ashore he spent his money lavishly on his celebrating shipmates.

The sailor Reuben James had been called before the ship's company and asked to name his reward for saving Decatur's life by offering his own in its stead. He grinned embarrassedly, a big, modest man, twisting his cap in his work-calloused hands.

"Well, sir," he said, after clearing his throat three times, "it's like this, sir. I've thought and thought on't, and there's nothing I'd ruther have than be excused from scrubbing hammocks for the rest of me days, sir!"

The officers laughed heartily at this, but a gasp of dismay went up from some of the crew, many of whom had been prompting the grizzled sailor to ask for a pension, a nice slice of cash, or even a promotion to petty officer. But Reuben James stubbornly held to his request: "Nay, sir, there's nothing more accursed than scrubbing those tarnation hammocks, and if 'twere not for that plaguey chore, why, a man might enjoy his life in the service!"

"It shall be done, then!" Decatur cried, still laughing. "From now on, Seaman James is to be excused from scrubbing hammocks — forever!"

In Syracuse, the rendezvous of the squadron, where Commodore Preble was dickering with the king of Sicily for some extra gunboats, Jack Griggs met with his old shipmate, Jethro Stubbs, who was on shore leave from the schooner *Nautilus*. There, with Catalano, the crew of the *Intrepid*, and other good companions, they all celebrated jubilantly together.

They climbed Mount Etna. They rode donkeys all over the island, and were smiled at wherever they went by the friendly inhabitants. They toasted one another in the grog shops of the harbor, and walked arm-in-arm, singing, up the crooked little streets where terrified hens and bleating goats scuttled out of their way. They bought the usual extravagances of sailors: golden earrings, lucky rings, stilettos, and an assortment of pets with which to while away lonely hours on shipboard — a donkey which ran away, a dancing bear which tore Reuben James's best muster trousers, and a parrot which rode about on Jack's shoulders, cursing in five languages.

It all came quickly enough to an end, however, and as they parted again Jethro Stubbs turned suddenly serious. "Well, Jack my lad, you've done your share for what you might call the family honor. I've a hunch my turn's coming up next. Lookit here, I've a bit of money put by. I've plans for us when this war's over — a nice ship on a hill, where you must set down awhile and get some book learning."

"Leave the sea?" Jack cried, incredulous, as though this were some kind of blasphemy. "Swallow the anchor?"

"You're young, Jack," said the red-bearded sailor, shaking his head. "But the sea soon eats up a man. The bad grub, the beatings, plague and accidents. How many old gray salts do you see busy about a ship's deck? Darn few! No, there's adventure awaiting ashore too, lad. We might head west if you like. There a man's his own man and none to whip him, none to lord it over him like a king!"

Jack Griggs had never heard his friend speak in such fashion. But he soon dismissed Stubbs's earnest talk as a fit of the blue devils. All sailors felt that way one time or another, but they never did anything about it.

The squadron was suddenly ordered back to Tripoli. Some big action was brewing. The commodore had wangled out of his ally, the king of Sicily, six small flat-bottomed gunboats and two heavy mortars, as well as a big store of ammunition.

Preble was feeling pleased with all his "boys," especially with young Decatur. When told of the firing of the *Philadelphia*, Lord Nelson pronounced it "the most bold and daring act of the age." The Old Man foresaw a brilliant career for his young officer, and sat down to write a glowing letter to Washington about him.

It was now midsummer. Soon the savage autumn storms would make any kind of action off the north coast of Africa impossible. So Preble thought now was the time to throw everything he had at the bashaw's head. On August third he gave the order to attack.

The bashaw was ready for the American fleet. He had in fact been watching their maneuvers for some time. Just outside the rocks and shoals that guarded the harbor he had stationed nineteen gunboats to meet them.

They moved in, six to the bashaw's nineteen, in a bold attack — the smaller ships ready to engage the gunboats in hand-to-hand battle, the frigate *Constitution* to cover their advance with heavy gunfire. The first shot from the frigate's Long Toms went as far as the bashaw's castle, impairing a section of wall. The crew cheered wildly, interpreting this as a good omen.

This was the first time the *Constitution* had actually been under fire. Her crew behaved well, those aloft working the canvas as though all the bashaw's forts were not blazing away at them, the gunners at their posts toiling feverishly in a sulfurous mist to keep up a heavy barrage.

Down on the sanded gun deck, the gunners worked frantically, half-naked bodies stained with sweat and black powder. They required incessant teamwork to keep the guns blazing. Each of the crew had to perform some part of the action in turn before the cumbersome cannon could be fired. The loaders crammed the charge, a six-pound sack of gunpowder, down the bore with a ramrod. After that they added the round shot, rusted from storage in the hold. Upon this they rammed a wad of frayed rope, to keep the shot from spilling before the gun went off. A man stood ready with a priming wire, which he thrust through a vent in the breech to puncture the sack of gunpowder. Into this hole another man spilled a quillful of powder, which was touched off by a slow match.

Now all was ready, and the gun was crudely aimed with quoin and tackle. The thunderous blast came next, causing a terrific recoil as the gun leaped backward on its wooden wheels. Men leaped nimbly out of the way of the dangerous recoil, which could cripple them, while others strained to check it by ropes and lashings.

Back and forth from gun crew to powder magazine ran the little powder monkeys, ducking under the woolen blanket that covered the door against stray sparks, scuttling out with the six-pound charge under their jackets, and racing back to the sweating gun crew, who seized it from them.

A heavy stray shot hit a gun on the port side. There was a deafening explosion as the gun burst, throwing huge fragments of iron into the air. Miraculously, after the smoke had cleared, only one man was found to be wounded.

Next, the ship's goat was beheaded as she calmly stood in her pen chewing some straw. And presently a little Portuguese powder monkey the ship had picked up in Lisbon was blown to bits with another stray shot as he was rushing back with his charge of gunpowder.

The heaviest fighting, however, was borne by the attacking party which had gone in to seize the gunboats. Decatur, Somers, and all the other young officers fought incessant hand-to-hand battles alongside their men as they tried to board and capture the enemy ships.

Near the end of the day they returned with three captured gunboats. The whole squadron moved out of range then, and Lieutenant Decatur came aboard the *Constitution*, pale and disheveled, to make his report to the commodore.

Although he had just won a considerable victory against heavy odds, young Decatur looked weary and depressed. He had just come from the ship where his brother, James, lay dying, wounded by enemy fire in the heavy bombardment. He went slowly toward Preble, saying, "Sir, I've brought you three enemy ships."

And then, in full sight of the ship's company, Preble did an astounding thing. To the victorious young officer he cried, "And why, sir, couldn't you have brought me a few more?"

He strode up to Decatur, took him by the shoulder, and shook him as though he were a dull schoolboy who could not remember his multiplication table.

Decatur recoiled. Abruptly he turned on his heel and strode off without a word.

In the fo'c'sle there was much talk about why the Old Man had behaved in this shameless fashion. Some said it was just plain cussedness; others, that he wanted to shock the young officer out of his grief. Whatever the reason, the commodore soon afterward sent for Decatur, and they were closeted together for several hours. The cabin boy reported they were sitting with clasped hands, weeping together like babies.

A few days later a second bombardment was under way. That evening, after the battle, the Americans sighted a Yankee frigate making toward them with all speed. It was the *John Adams* with a message for Preble from Washington: a new squadron was on its way under Commodore Barron, who would take over.

The news depressed the Old Man. The men were sorry. They argued that he had done a fairly good job with few ships and little support. Why, he wasn't such a bad sort, at that. His bark was worse than his bite. He seemed sick — maybe that accounted for his temper. He often clutched himself as if in pain. But he was brave, and what he knew about ships he had learned the hard way.

Until the new commodore arrived, Preble remained in charge. He wanted to get in as many parting shots as he could before the weather turned bad. He concentrated heavy fire on the harbor again, attacking with his entire squadron of gunboats, brigs, and schooners.

In this third engagement off Tripoli the *Constitution* performed daring acts. She moved in close to the dangerous rocks where the ill-fated *Philadelphia* had gone aground, and with every gun in the harbor blazing away at her she sank one enemy ship, drove two others aground, and scattered the rest single-handed. But she had come so close to the shore batteries that this time even the wretched gunnery of the Tripolitans was effective. Her sails were shot to ribbons, her rigging badly damaged. Her figurehead — Hercules, with a scroll representing the Bill of Rights in one hand and an uplifted club in the other — was also shot away. But her crew

Detail of "Battle of Tripoli," by Michel F. Corne. (U.S. Naval Academy Museum, Annapolis)

claimed she was a lucky ship, for in all this heavy fire her losses remained light. Her masts never fell, and her hull was undamaged.

September was now at hand, with its squally weather. Preble was low on stores and ammunition. Any day now Barron would arrive with his rival fleet to take over operations. Before Preble left, he wanted to perform one last act of daring — a surprise action, like the burning of the *Philadelphia*. So he and his officers together devised another plan to make use of the heroic little ketch, the *Intrepid*.

Lieutenant Richard Somers, that mild and gentle officer, was to take the ketch into Tripoli harbor once again under cover of night and sail right up under the bashaw's castle. But this time she would serve as a mine ship. Crammed to the scuppers with explosives, the ketch would blow up, damage the castle and shore batteries, and sink or cripple scores of ships anchored nearby. The hand-picked party of three officers and ten men counted on getting away in a small boat, aided by the confusion that would follow the explosion.

One of the ten picked to man the ketch was Jethro Stubbs. Jack could see his friend at work during loading operations, the sailor's red head and beard flaming in the hot sun. He waved joyously to Johnny, but the ketch never came within hailing distance of the *Constitution*.

As the sun dipped out of sight, the *Intrepid*, packed with all the barrels of gunpowder and loaded shells she could carry, moved off to make her way alone into the harbor. The whole squadron watched anxiously as she vanished into deepening darkness. Tensely they waited for the explosion.

It came much sooner than they had anticipated.

Just outside the harbor entrance there was a sudden great burst, an uprush of blinding light. A thunderous sound shook the heavy masts of the *Constitution*. Evidently the little ketch had not been able to get inside the harbor.

But Seaman Jack Griggs, whose eyes were young and keen and who had been prayerfully watching the spot where the ketch vanished into darkness, saw one brief, swift scene before the terrifying explosion came: a man running with a lantern, leaping down a lighted hatchway where the powder was stored.

Morning revealed no trace of the *Intrepid* anywhere — not a splinter of wood, not a drowned body floating in with the tide along the rocky shoals. What had happened? Had the mine ship accidentally exploded? Or had she been discovered, and had brave Somers given the order to blow her up rather than be captured?

There was never any explanation. Only young Jack remembered his vision. He could have sworn that as the man with the lantern leaped into the hatchway, his head and beard flamed vivid red. Jack liked to think that this was so — that it was his last glimpse of his friend, the best friend he had had or would ever have again.

After this tragedy the weather turned bleak and stormy. Soon the new commodore arrived with the frigates *President* and *Constellation*, bringing a reward for brave Decatur — a commission as captain. And Commodore Preble left for home in the *John Adams*.

Jack Griggs was also able to get passage home. He had had enough of the sea — well, for a while, maybe. Perhaps his friend had had a presentiment when he had spoken to Jack so earnestly about book learning. He had had plans. The least Jack could do, he thought, was to carry them out himself.

He kept hearing the voice of the red-bearded sailor:

"You're young, Jack . . . But the sea soon eats up a man . . ."

It was true. Young as he was, he could see that it was so. No stone marked the grave of the crew of the *Intrepid*. They lay in the everlasting deep, along with the *Philadelphia*.

To the end of his days Commodore Preble remained an embittered man. But it was owing almost entirely to his efforts that in the following spring, in the year 1805, Tunis and Tripoli both signed treaties of peace with the United States.

As for the last of the Barbary states, Algiers, it was dealt with later, in 1815. Thus the two-hundred-year rule of the pirates who preyed on merchant ships and lived on the ransom of their captives was finally broken forever.

Part Two

CHAPTER VII

Mutiny!

*I*N THE AUTUMN of 1805 the crew of the *Constitution* was in a sullen frame of mind. The war with Tunis and Tripoli was over. Many of the men had been due home long before. Still no relief ship came to take those whose time was up back to the States. Some of them had signed up for three years and had been away as long as four.

The ship remained in the Mediterranean, having nothing in particular to do. And to lower the morale of the crew further, unpopular officers plagued them.

Nobody knew where Commodore Rodgers had managed to obtain his first lieutenant, Mr. Blake. Some claimed he was a renegade Englishman, thrown out of the British navy for skullduggery. His face was long and thin. His lips were mean. His methods were those of a bucko mate on the worst hellship that ever put out for death and disaster. He would give a sailor three dozen with the cat for a trifling offense that rated nothing more serious than having his grog stopped. If he didn't think the lash bit deeply enough into a man's flayed back, he would seize the bloody cat-o'-nine-tails and perform the flogging himself. And to boot he would thrash the man who had failed to perform the whipping to his satisfaction.

The heartiest and most fanciful curses were reserved for Lieutenant Blake when the men talked about him in the fo'c'sle. The fact that many of the men's terms of service had expired and thus, they argued, the officers had no more authority to whip them added to their bitterness.

Then one of their messmates tried to jump ship. He was caught and of course court-martialed, and forced to undergo the torture of being whipped through the fleet — a common enough sight in the British navy. This cruel punishment meant that the man was stripped to the waist and, with his arms lashed fast to a wooden gallows, was taken from ship to ship in a small boat. Another boat, full of musicians, followed him on his rounds, playing the "Rogue's March." At each ship the unhappy wretch received part of his punishment, a total of three hundred lashes when he had circled the fleet. After this, if he was still alive, he was put in the ship's hospital and forgiven.

Sadly enough, such a man was never much use afterward. And when a ship's company had to watch one of their own messmates undergoing this torture, they could feel only pity for him, no matter how much of a rogue he might have been.

The poor wretch who had deserted the *Constitution* managed to survive. But the men were greatly depressed, blaming the bad state of affairs, and Lieutenant Blake in particular, for driving him to desertion.

And then, to everyone's relief, they managed to get rid of the sinister Mr. Blake. The *Essex* met them, took him aboard, and gave them in exchange a new first lieutenant, a Mr. Ludlow. They had a new captain too, Captain Campbell, while Commodore Rodgers went home in the *Essex*. Relations were somewhat better, but the wounds that Lieutenant Blake had left were still rankling.

The men thought that the *Essex* had come to replace them, but still no relief was in sight. Without a word about when they would sail for home they were sent back to make yet another round of the Mediterranean.

The weather grew wild. They were caught in the famous levantine winds blowing from Africa. In a terrific gale the *Constitution* took a considerable battering and had to put in at Malta for extensive repairs. And it was here, lying off Malta, that a mutiny occurred.

No one had any thought of mutiny when, on a bright, sunny day that was warm for the time of the year, the deck officer, Burroughs, gave permission for all hands to go overside and bathe in the ocean. Captain Campbell was ashore on business. The ship was in the hands of its officers. Happy as children at having something pleasant to do, the men gamboled and clowned in the water as they went about their ablutions. One of them broke away from the rest and swam off from the ship with quick, vigorous strokes.

A British frigate was at anchor some distance away. The American officers were nervous because there had been considerable friction of late. Men grumbled aloud. When drunk, they were apt to be abusive. Perhaps the officer thought that the swimmer, who swam as far as the British ship's buoy, where he stopped, was attempting desertion. The officer angrily ordered him back, and when he did not return sent one of his shipmates to fetch him.

When the two dripping swimmers stepped aboard deck, breathing hard, Burroughs tersely ordered the boatswain's mate to get the cat and flog the first man for disobedience.

"What for, sir?" demanded the sailor. "I've done naught. The waves were slapping about and making a great noise, and I never heard you."

"You are lying!" Burroughs accused. "You were making for the British frigate as fast as you could swim. Take off your shirt, and stand and be flogged!"

The sailor lowered his head. Uncertainly he plucked at his sodden undershirt. His chest heaved belligerently. He made no move to obey the order.

"Ye'd be a fool to peel off your shirt and take the rope's end for nothing!" put in the man who had brought him to the ship, nudging him from behind. "Stand firm for your rights!"

A tenseness like the queer, prickly feeling before an electrical storm pervaded the ship. Most of the crew had clambered aboard, hastily pulling on trousers and jackets. They crowded about, looking sullen and threatening.

"I'll not be flogged!" the man suddenly shouted, clenching his large, hairy hands. "Come at me with your fists if you like, like a man! But you've no more rights to hold a whip over John Smith!"

There were cries of "Hear, hear!" "That's right!" and "Speak up!" from the crew witnessing this open defiance.

Burroughs's face turned white. Biting his underlip, he turned upon the boatswain's mate and curtly ordered, "Seize them both up, and flog them for insolence!"

The boatswain's mate stood by with the pronged whip dangling in his hands. He too looked sullen and defiant. "Nay, that I'll not do," he said, shaking his head. "'Twas an unjust order in the first place."

A cheer broke out from the crew, and the men suddenly milled around the officer and the two men. Some confusion followed. Afterward, some claimed that Lieutenant Burroughs had lifted a handspike against Seaman Smith. Others said that he had struck at the boatswain with his fist, and the boatswain had seized a crowbar. At any rate, Burroughs clambered up on one of the cannon. There he was standing as if at bay when the first lieutenant came rushing on deck.

Pale, his face contorted, the besieged Burroughs shouted, "Put these men into irons!"

But now the crew was completely out of hand, crying, "Let them go!" "We demand a hearing!" "We'll deal with none but the captain!"

The officers retreated then to the quarter-deck. A rumor blazed about the ship that Lieutenant Ludlow had asked the Marines to fire on the men and the captain of the Marines had refused. True or false, this rumor once again threw the whole crew into nervous confusion. Here and there men shouted, "The cowards!" and "To the forecastle!"

With swords and pistols the officers appeared again and ordered that the men be piped down to their hammocks. Then, on pain of death, every man was ordered supperless to bed. Seaman Smith, the man who had urged Smith to defy the officer, and the boatswain's mate who had refused to flog him were put in irons under officers' guard.

All hands turned in, sullen but obedient. The news had gone about that Lieutenant Ludlow had sent for the captain. The men stayed quietly in their hammocks under guard, waiting to see what the captain would do.

When Captain Campbell came aboard in great haste,

he looked sharply at the lieutenant, seeing the officers on deck fully armed. The light burned all night in his cabin as one officer after another came to make his report. Occasionally the men could hear the captain's voice raised in anger. Few of the crew slept, and those who did slept fitfully. In the morning, they learned that the entire crew was under arrest for mutiny.

Mutiny was a serious crime. Next only to murder, it rated the highest punishment at sea. British captains had mutinous men keelhauled: the brutal torture of dragging a man under a ship's belly, where the barnacles cut him to pieces if he wasn't lucky enough to drown. More usually mutineers were whipped through the fleet, or sometimes hung from the yardarm under a yellow flag.

The sun was well up next morning before the crew of the frigate were piped out of their hammocks and mustered on deck. But Captain Campbell, standing on the quarter-deck, spoke to them in a cheerful voice: "Men!"

At the tone of his voice, several downcast faces lifted.

"The purser has made out a list of those whose service has expired. These are to remain here. The rest are dismissed."

Part of the crew walked off. To the others the captain said, "Now state your grievances."

Nudged by the rest, a man stepped forward to the captain's mast. The ship's armorer, he had undertaken to be spokesman for the crew. One by one he enumerated the things the men felt to be abuses. He told the captain that men had been thrashed months after their term of service had expired. They were long overdue in the States, and they would go quietly under the captain's command if he would give the order to sail the *Constitution* home.

"And if I do not?" the captain asked.

"Nay, then we must consider ourselves our own men, no longer at your command."

"Well, if you've a mind to take over the ship and take the consequences, then you may. But if you will be patient awhile longer, I'll go about my business with all speed. And from now on, I promise, no man shall be punished unless he deserves it."

The three prisoners remained in irons while the frigate continued on its rounds. Captain Campbell did seem to be hurrying his business, yet instead of being homeward bound, the men were making for more and more distant Italian ports. One more incident occurred when the captain attempted to put in at Messina and the men refused to lower the sails. In an uneasy state, the crew finally put the ship about and proceeded toward the Strait of Gibraltar.

Off Málaga, news came that a British ship, the *Leopard*, had fired on the Yankee frigate *Chesapeake*, and that the Yankee frigate had struck her colors. After scarcely a struggle the *Chesapeake* had allowed the captain of the

Leopard to come aboard her and remove four of her men. Three were Yankees, two of them blacks. The fourth was British but had enlisted under a false name. They were dragged off by force while their captain stood by helplessly.

This incident was actually the first hostile act of the War of 1812.

Anxiously Captain Campbell tried to ascertain whether a state of war existed between England and America. And if war had broken out, could he count on his mutinous crew?

He had the crew mustered on deck and went to speak to them himself. "Men," he told them, "you have had a long voyage — for many of you, longer than you bargained for. But we're approaching the straits and at last, I hope, we'll be on our way home!"

At the word *home* the men broke into a cheer. They had not seen home for four years.

"But this very minute," the captain went on, "we may be at war with England. We are approaching Gibraltar. The British fleet is lying there. Men, if I mount four more cannon, would you fight your way home if need be?"

The men looked at one another uneasily. Now, with their morale at lowest ebb, they were faced with the prospect of war and sudden death far from home waters. Who knew now when they would get home? Perhaps some of them never would. Even the oldest sailors, men tough enough to survive a lifetime on the sea, looked glum.

Then a man spoke out: "Why be downhearted, mates? The best girl's on the towrope! We're homeward bound — and home we'll go. Let anyone try and stop us now!"

This simple appeal swayed the mood of the men. Home was still far away, but they would fight their way through all the navies of the world to get there. A cheer broke out, ragged at first, then swelling stronger and stronger.

"We'll fight!" they cried. "We'll fight!"

And so the frigate, alerted for war, came in sight of Ape's Hill and passed through the Strait of Gibraltar. But at Gibraltar her men found no war after all. And a little later a Yankee ship met them with orders to make for America with all speed. So the *Constitution* at last ended her long Mediterranean cruise and headed for home, where she remained, in American waters, until the eve of 1812.

CHAPTER VIII

Mr. Madison's War

*A*MOS BROWN enlisted in the spring of 1811. The oldest of a brood of six, he had walked all the way to Boston from his father's backwoods farm, which had gone bankrupt in the depression that followed the Embargo Act of 1807.

Times were hard. Farmers could not sell their crops of corn, tobacco, or hemp. Trade by land or by sea had been cut off, and the young country choked on its own produce. The falling markets brought falling prices. In the rich valleys of the Ohio, the Cumberland, and the Tennessee, many a pioneer farmer could not meet his mortgage. In the big cities, countinghouses went into bankruptcy. Ships were idle at the wharves, and seamen could not get jobs.

The Embargo Act had been repealed by Congress in 1809. But the harm it had done was still felt. Relations with England and her colonies were at their lowest since the Revolutionary War. It seemed that circumstances would lead very soon to another war.

"Amos," his mother told him, "there's nothing for you to do but go to Boston and try to get a berth on a ship. Zeke's going to the new woolen mill. Pa and me and the young 'uns are going to Cousin Cary's. Maybe Pa can get enough work in the lumber mill there to keep us all alive. We can't keep this place any longer."

"But it's the best crop we've had in many a season," Amos said.

"It's arotting in the barn, Amos." His mother sighed. "There's no one to buy it."

So Amos put away his squirrel gun, his traps, and his musket and walked all the way to Boston.

He found the city buzzing with bewildering talk. Folks said war was coming sure enough, and it was all Mr. James Madison's doing. The people of Boston and of New England generally were hostile to the President's party of "war hawks."

The Boston papers were bitter against President Madison for provoking a war with England at this time. England, they said, was fighting the tyrant Napoleon; why should the United States be her enemy? Were we not with her in such a struggle? Others pointed out that the young country was still paying off the debts that it had incurred in the Revolutionary War; why, then, should we go looking for another war? And besides, England's mighty navy could blockade American coastal cities and starve us to death. Our navy consisted of only sixteen first-class fighting ships. Could they defend our ports against invasion?

But in the boarding house where Amos stayed three days he met a man who showed him a Philadelphia paper with a flaming headline: "Remember the *Chesapeake!*" And Amos read there that the impressment of American seamen by British captains had gone beyond any endurance.

"Where is our national honor?" the editor asked. "We cannot defend our own citizens!" He wrote further that trade was the lifeline of the country, and that America must become a first-class sea power to survive, even if it meant fighting England. And the man told Amos that in New York and Philadelphia the people supported a war with England.

But Amos truly did not know the right or wrong of it. He felt confused by all this talk of war and politics. He was a backwoods boy, simple, plainspoken, and straightforward. His extremely long arms stuck out of his homespun clothes in an awkward fashion. He knew how to shoot, to track game, to set traps, and to work the land. But now times were hard and he was off the land, looking for a job along the Boston wharves.

The very first day he discovered there was no way of getting a berth in the merchant marine. There were too many skilled seamen looking for work. The pay was lower in the navy, and the risk was greater, too, because of the danger of war. But there a green backwoods boy like him had a chance.

To his great joy, the navy recruiting officer accepted him, and he was given a uniform. On the recruiting ship, an old, disabled hulk, he stumbled about awkwardly trying to learn this strange new world of ropes and rigging — a trackless forest where he did not know the way.

From the recruiting ship he stepped aboard the decks of the *Constitution*.

Even on his remote farm he had heard about the gallant frigate, and now that he was actually aboard her he had a feeling of awe. He looked about the bustling scene of loading and making ready to sail, half-smiling at the idea of great adventures in store for him, things to tell his brother Zeke and Ma and Pa and the rest when he saw them again. He looked up, admiring the soaring masts as tall as the tallest pines he had ever seen, and thinking of how they had once grown in forests and how deer had nestled in their shade.

Someone pulled his sleeve. A ship's boy stood before him, a pug-nosed little powder monkey who told him, "Old Switchell sez you're to tend the cap'n's garden."

"Who's Old Switchell?" Amos asked innocently.

"Cap'n Isaac Hull, of course! Everybody calls him that 'cause he drinks switchell — molasses and water. He sez you're to tend his garden and go up forward and report."

Commodore Isaac Hull.
(Peabody Museum of Salem)

Amos brightened. If the captain kept a garden and if Amos was to tend it, then he would not be unhandy and laughed at for mistakes. This would be something he could do and do well. He saw Captain Hull forward, where the little powder monkey pointed, and went toward him.

In his simplicity Amos did not hear the snickers and elaborate coughing that broke out along the way. The sailors turned aside as he passed by, some wiping tears from their eyes. The pug-nosed boy who had sent him doubled up like a jackknife.

Captain Isaac Hull, the commander of the *Constitution*, was talking to his first lieutenant, Charles Morris. Short, thickset, bluff in manner, and rather plain-featured, the captain for all that had something about him that appealed to Amos.

"Cap'n Hull, sir," Amos said, "I've come to report."

Hull's eyebrows met. "Who in blazes sent you here?" he snapped.

"Why, sir, I'm the one to tend your garden, sir — "

"My *what*? Suffering catfish, man, what d'ye think shipboard life is? You're on a ship, not a sarse-patch! Hey, you!" the captain bawled at a seaman working nearby. "Take this green bushwhacker to blazes out of my sight! Show him about, rub some of the moss off him! And remember, now — any more horseplay and the one responsible gets five at the gangway. Understand?"

A thickset sailor with sandy hair and short legs came up, took the red-faced, confused Amos by the arm, and pulled him hastily away.

When they were out of earshot of the captain, the sailor spat over the rail and introduced himself. "Name's Ferrrgusson. And you'll not forget that John Paul Jones was likewise Scottish. Now that we've had our bit of joke, and no harm done, come aft here and meet your topmates."

Bill Fergusson showed him his hammock and locker and had him meet the others of his work gang.

There was a one-eared sailor with a most lugubrious face who was known as Smiley. It was said that he was an ex-smuggler.

There was a seaman, six foot four, lithe as a bobcat, with polished skin as black as the newly oiled cannon. The men called him Long Tom.

There was Moses Smith, a brawny sailor who read books and sat writing notes in an exercise book. The men said he was writing his memoirs and teased him incessantly about it.

The pug-nosed boy who had sent Amos to Captain Hull was named Danny Hoagan. He and the other ship's boys played an endless and rather perilous game of follow-the-leader, scrambling up the fighting tops and sliding down the backstays. Skylarking, it was called. It seemed that the agile little powder monkeys were always at it, and Amos could only admire their nerve and agility. They were as at home aloft as squirrels in a treetop — while Amos was so awkward that, the very first day out of Boston, he felt a whip on his back for the first time in his life, for bungling a reef in the foresail.

He went supperless to bed for his mistake, but Long Tom came over to him with some hardtack and bully beef his messmates had saved for him, and a little grog. Amos fell asleep feeling glad and somehow warm in spite of his sore back.

The ship stopped at Annapolis to collect the rest of the crew, and took aboard a few more black recruits. And there news came of a new incident at sea with the British. The *John Adams* had come back from overseas with a story that captured the imagination of all the

Baltimore papers, and for days the crew of the *Constitution* could talk of little else.

A black sailor had escaped from a British ship and taken refuge aboard the *John Adams*. He had papers proving he was a Yankee from New York, so the captain of the *John Adams* tried to protect him. But when the British came aboard looking for the runaway, the captain was forced to give the man up. The sailor wept and begged not to be taken into a foreign service. But there was nothing the captain of the *John Adams* could do. The British officers dragged the man away, weeping and protesting. Faced with certain punishment for desertion, he broke loose from his captors and, in plain sight of all the crew of the *John Adams*, seized a boarding axe from its rack and chopped off the fingers of his right hand. Even this heroic act did not save him from impressment. He was taken off anyway, to what fate no one knew.

Aboard the *Constitution*, the men gathered around Long Tom and the other black sailors. They remembered that, of the four men taken from the *Chesapeake* when she was fired upon by the *Leopard* in 1807, two were blacks. The incident on the *John Adams* captured everyone's sympathy and threw the black sailors into prominence. Men who had been a bit aloof in their manner to Long Tom now came and warmly shook his hand. His workmates were proud of him.

"A most noble African," said Moses Smith of the

sailor on the *John Adams*. "Indeed, where is the man among us who would do as much?"

Thus, in most uneasy times the *Constitution* put to sea.

News traveled so slowly that war might break out before those aboard ship heard of it. Every British man-of-war they might meet on their voyage was a potential enemy who might fire on them first.

Captain Hull had been entrusted with transporting money to Holland to repay the Dutch for ammunition they had supplied during the Revolutionary War. The crew's journey took them through English waters to British ports. Still, nothing eventful occurred.

To Amos Brown, however, the journey was crammed full of adventure. The frigate encountered terrific storms in the mid-Atlantic, and the men had to work aloft in a gale, clinging to the yardarm, hands numb and clothes sodden and chill, as the ship pitched below. They lost a man from Amos's work gang — sad-faced Smiley, who fell into the sea and vanished amid the swells and driving rain.

And there was a terrifying day when Amos went dispiritedly about his tasks, suddenly feeling feverish and chill at the same time. Long Tom took a good look at his dazed, glassy eyes and yelled, "This man has the plague!"

The men grabbed Amos and hurried him to sick bay. A nightmare followed. At one time Amos believed that he was in hell. Choking smoke, brimstone, and a terrifying odor were all about him.

The plague took several men. It was swift and usually certain. Men became ill in the morning. By night they were sewn into their hammocks with a penny from their shipmates, the traditional "fare for Charon," between their teeth.

There was no known cure for ship's fever, nor was it known what caused the mysterious plague that sometimes decimated a crew at sea. Some thought it might have something to do with rats and other vermin. Someone had noticed that when a ship was fumigated the plague sometimes abated, so the crew smoked the *Constitution* out with sulfur to rid it of pests.

Cupping and bleeding was all the ship's surgeon could do for Amos. This weakened him terribly, but he was young and tough, and he managed to survive the primitive medical care of his day. Once on his feet again, he mended rapidly. By the time he reached England Amos was in as good shape as he had ever been. Several faces were missing, but none of his own gang had been touched by the plague.

At Portsmouth, England, a man from Amos's work crew deserted. He was an unpleasant creature who had been assigned to replace the unfortunate Smiley. He sneered at Long Tom and had been heard to remark that he did not care to work alongside a savage.

Bill Fergusson told the newcomer to "go batten his

hatch" and muttered that he was "the kind of rapscallion that'd lock his sea chest" — a great crime among sailors, who never stole from one another. They believed that only a thief would have so little trust in his fellowmen as to keep his chest under lock and key.

The other men also failed to warm up to the new-comer. When he swam off to a British frigate, the *Havannah*, that was anchored nearby, Amos was glad to see him go. But Captain Hull was furious. They were short-handed as it was because of the plague, so an officer was sent to fetch him back. The captain of the *Havannah* and the admiral of the fleet both refused to give up the *Constitution*'s man.

That same night a man with Yankee papers deserted from the very ship on which the *Constitution*'s man had taken refuge. The new deserter fastened wooden blocks beneath his arms and floated on the tide. The frigate's crew took him aboard, and when the British officers came to claim him, Hull sent Lieutenant Morris, who refused to let them even see the deserter.

"Tit for tat," said Hull. "They've got my man, I've got theirs. I'll not give him up though the devil himself comes aboard looking for him!"

He appealed to the men. "What d'you say, boys — are you ready to fight if they try to take him off?"

The whole crew cheered. Even the men in irons for drunkenness and other crimes cheered and were fired by Hull's defiant words.

The British fleet lying at Portsmouth was agog at the incident. Hull ordered battle lanterns lit and told the gun crews to stand by the guns and exercise them "just a little, to warm 'em up, in case." But the British did not return for their man, and the *Constitution* managed to leave Portsmouth without hindrance.

Hull delivered the payment to Holland and then turned the *Constitution* homeward. They were back at Annapolis, nine months to the day after Amos Brown enlisted, when President Madison issued his proclamation of war.

CHAPTER IX

Hounds of the Sea

*W*AR WAS DECLARED on June 18, 1812. The country received the news soberly. Though England's main struggle was in Europe with Napoleon, she still had fleets of men-of-war hovering off the Atlantic coast. The people of Baltimore feared that their city might be bombarded or even invaded. A kind of panic swept the coastal cities.

As the *Constitution* sailed proudly down Chesapeake Bay on her way to join the American squadron at New York, the people of Baltimore, Norfolk, and Portsmouth turned out to cheer her. She was in good hands. Old Switchell — Captain Isaac Hull — and his second-in-command, Lieutenant Charles Morris, were both veterans of the storming of Tripoli. All along the way people felt a bit more reassured, a little bit heartened by the graceful sight of the famous fighting frigate.

The *Constitution* headed for New York harbor, but

there the way was barred by a British squadron block-
ading the port. She turned aside then and began cruising
about on her own.

On a hot July afternoon somewhere off Barnegat Bay,
the lookout in the maintop sang out, "Sail ho!"

Old Switchell himself came out of his cabin to have a
look, and after studying the stranger keenly through the
glass, he ordered the crew to give chase. The stranger
fled from them throughout the night. The men slept
beside their guns, ready for action if necessary.

When daylight came Amos, who was stationed at one
of the main-deck guns, sleepily rubbed his eyes and
looked about him. There were now not one, but seven
ships in sight! During the night, the frigate had managed
to overtake an entire squadron.

The men rushed to the rail. Shading their eyes, they
speculated about the strange ships.

"They're men-of-war, all right," said Bill Fergusson.
"They *may* be Yankees, though. May be our own squadron. It could be that they ran the blockade and got away
to sea."

The spyglasses showed four frigates, a ship of the line,
a schooner, and a brig. All seemed heavily armed. They
had crowded on every spare scrap of sail, and the entire
squadron was now bearing down on the *Constitution*.

A cry from the maintop electrified the entire ship:
"They're British! The *Shannon*'s nearest! And next in
line is the *Guerrière*!"

"Beat to quarters!" Hull shouted. "Stand by, men, to fight if we're overtaken!"

Every man went scurrying to his battle station. The officers went up and down the line checking the gun crews. The gun captains responded with, "All ready, sir!" Then all was quiet aboard the frigate, every man waiting for what would happen next.

The *Shannon* and the *Guerrière* were rapidly gaining, wind and current both being in their favor. From his station on the main deck Amos saw the ensign flying from the topmast of the nearest ship — the Cross of St. George, white on a red field. The ship was still out of gunshot range but was coming in closer and closer. Hull ordered a gun fired to serve notice that he was prepared to stand and fight if overtaken.

Boom! The *Constitution* hurled her challenge. The *Shannon* instantly returned it. A moment later the *Guerrière*'s signal gun flashed red.

And then, as luck would have it, the light and fitful winds that had been favoring the pursuers ceased altogether. The sails hung slack. The sea became still as glass. All were becalmed, hunters and hunted alike. Not a puff of air, not a cloud appeared in the hot July sky.

Now there's nothing for it but to sweat it out, thought Amos, wiping his moist brow. He looked aloft anxiously. The loose sails hung in listless folds about the masts, giving the ship a somewhat dejected air. A bluish haze in the distance might have been the New Jersey coast.

On the quarter-deck Hull and his officers held anxious consultation, for though there was no wind, the British ships were drifting closer. The current favored the *Shannon* and the *Guerrière*. The Americans watched anxiously, helpless, while three miles shortened to two. One more mile to go, and then they would come within firing range of the *Shannon*'s big guns.

"Try the sweeps," Hull ordered.

The crew applied themselves to the back-breaking task of moving the frigate along with sweeps. But this did not help. The *Shannon* also got out sweeps and, aided by the rapid drift of the current, bore down remorselessly upon them. Again her bow guns snarled a challenge. It was as if she derided their feeble efforts to get away from her.

"Now what's Old Switchell going to do?" Amos remarked to his sweating neighbor, a sailor with bushy hair and beard who was pulling and grunting alongside him at the sweeps.

"He's sure got to be smart to get out of *this* fix," the sailor replied.

Old Switchell was indeed in a very tight spot. The next time the *Shannon*'s guns blazed, they would be within range. It was true that fighting ships could not inflict any real damage unless they were grappled close. But while the helpless *Constitution* was standing off the *Shannon*, the other ships of the British squadron would come drifting in one by one until they had surrounded and captured her. Hull's thoughts were pretty grim as he saw that, no matter how his men toiled and how the sweeps bent with strain, the *Constitution* was steadily and surely losing the race.

"Captain Hull, sir," said Lieutenant Morris, "I think we should try kedging. An old commander of mine once warped our ship in and out of harbor with no wind. It should give us a speed of three knots, sir, which will more than offset the drift of the current. I think it may be our only chance."

"We'll try it," said Hull. "Get all the spare rope together! Order all hands to splice rope!"

So the men abandoned the sweeps, and in great haste assembled and spliced together all the spare rope aboard. It made a coil at least a mile long. The kedge anchor, a light anchor used for steadying the ship, was attached to one end of the rope. A crew was assigned to man a small boat and haul the anchor out to sea. They took it out a mile, the full length of the rope, and dropped it into the sea.

And then, back aboard the frigate, the laborious operation of kedging began. The crew hauled on the other end of the rope. This was done by "walking aft." The work crew lined up in single file, each man grasping the rope and hauling upon it as he strained to move aft of the vessel. When he reached the end he let go and ran forward to seize the rope again.

"Pull, my lads! Heave, my hearts of oak!" Hull cried. "All together now, and get her under way!"

The ship was moving — moving by sheer muscle

toward the kedge anchor and the waiting boat. With a creaking and straining, the frigate pulled away from the *Shannon*.

Amos, pausing a moment to look, saw the gap between the ships widen. He broke into a cheer which the men took up.

"We're doing it, lads!" cried Hull. "We're getting away!"

Long Tom, who was just in front of Amos, turned around and smiled. His splendid muscles rippled. His naked back was polished by sweat. He seemed tireless. When the first gang was ordered to fall out, he insisted on working a second shift.

The ship's bow came up to the anchor. The *Shannon* had now fallen back about half a mile. The Americans raised the anchor, took it out to sea again, and repeated the whole laborious operation.

They had barely gotten the anchor out when they saw small boats putting out from the *Shannon* and the *Guerrière*. Hull raised the spyglass and watched. Seeing that their quarry was getting away, the British had begun kedging too.

"So it's to be a kedging race," Hull muttered. "Mount cannon in the stern!" he ordered. "Give 'em a few parting shots! It may help propel the ship. And bring the spare kedge anchor. Divide all the rope in half and operate two kedges. Order out all the ship's boats and man them with crews."

And now the crew of the *Constitution* set their teeth for a really grim, dogged race in the blistering heat of the July sun. They towed the kedges out one after the other. As soon as they drew the ship's head up to one, they put the other in its place, ready for operation. That way, not a moment of time was lost. The crew aboard hauled continuously, two gangs alternating. All the ship's boats were now engaged in towing the anchors. And, by dint of muscle and sweat and heavy toil, the *Constitution* barely managed to hold her lead.

The sea was still dead calm. The flat, level shore of New Jersey was now plainly in sight.

"You know," said a sailor to Amos, "it looks like we c'd be cut off. Leastways, we can't tow much farther in this direction. We'd better whistle up a wind, for it looks like we're getting into a tight corner."

All the boats of the entire British squadron were now busily engaged in towing the two nearest ships. The *Constitution* began to lose her precarious lead. When the sun went down in a trail of crimson, the *Shannon* was closing in on them again.

With the coming of twilight a light breeze from land riffled the ocean. Hull quickly ordered the men aloft to shake out the sails. Wet canvas holds a wind best, so in order to take fullest advantage of every slight puff, the men formed brigades and passed buckets of water aloft to wet the sails.

And so, hour after hour through the night, the crew

"*Constitution* Escaping the British Squadron." Painting by George C. Wales. (Peabody Museum of Salem)

toiled on. When there was a bit of wind sails were shaken out and the canvas wetted. When the wind failed, kedging was resumed.

It was a red dawn. A strange, infernal sun rose from the glassy sea. A gory light spread over the ocean. Hull, anxiously pacing the quarter-deck, raised his spyglass to his weary eyes and counted four new ships that had joined the squadron in the night. The ships had changed positions. Now the *Shannon* had fallen back and the *Belvidera* was nearest, crowding them from a new quarter.

Not a man aboard had shut his eyes throughout the

night. Hull wondered how long his weary crew could keep up the exhausting strain. And yet no one thought of giving up.

The day wore on. The toil seemed endless. Hauling and straining, then up aloft to wet the sails. Then hauling again, then scrambling wearily along the yards, passing the brine-filled buckets.

Amos rubbed his red eyes. He passed his long fingers through his damp hair. He could feel a cool wind. He looked about him dazedly. Would it hold? The men drank it in greedily. It dried their sweating skin, refreshed their weary bodies.

Now they had a breather, for the ship was speeding along under its own sails. The wind was actually stiffening. The ship began to waggle and toss on long, heavy swells. The rising wind made a weird moan in the rigging, which seemed to Amos the pleasantest sound he had ever heard.

They were fleeing now under power of the wind, and the whole British squadron was speeding in pursuit.

"Say, lads," cried Moses Smith, pointing to some low, inky clouds that had burst suddenly over the horizon. "Get out your web feet! Wet weather coming up fast!"

The sea grew dark. Lightning flashed. A peal of thunder shook the ship.

"Topmen aloft!"

Up along the bucking yards the crew scrambled. Hurriedly they stripped the masts to make ready for the storm. The boats were taken in and lashed fast.

Aboard the *Belvidera* sailors were making similar preparations to ride out the storm. But the British had so many small boats bobbing about on the wild sea that time was lost getting them in. At the last moment, just before the storm struck, they had to cast some adrift.

The men aboard the *Constitution* had barely gotten the frigate ready when the storm broke. For a few moments the *Belvidera* remained visible, tossing about on the heaving sea, her crew still aloft reefing and furling the sails. Then, as the rain lashed in a terrific downpour, she was hidden behind a wall of mist.

"Now, my lads!" cried Hull, rubbing his hands exultantly. "Loose the mains'l! Set the t'gallants! Mr. Helmsman, down helm and let her run free! And while they think we're still lying to, we'll be halfway to Boston — before they ever miss us!"

The men scrambled aloft in the storm, soaking and blinded. They shook out and spread the storm-drenched sails. The wind's impact upon these sails was like a giant fist. Up and away leaped the frigate, like a wild deer bolting over a meadow. She ran before the wind at the speed of eleven knots.

She had had an hour of wild flight when the squall stopped as suddenly as it had begun. The sun came out and soaked up the mist. Far away on the horizon, a strip of white sail showed for a moment or two, and then went under.

CHAPTER X

"Old Ironsides"

*I*N BOSTON Captain Hull found a challenge awaiting him. It had been copied from London newspapers and was prominently displayed in all the Boston taverns.

A CHALLENGE

Captain Dacres, commander of his Britannic Majesty's frigate *Guerrière*, of 44 guns, presents his compliments to Commodore Rodgers, of the U.S. frigate *President*, and will be very happy to meet him, or any American frigate of equal force to the *President*, off Sandy Hook, for the purpose of having a few minutes tête–à–tête.

The *Guerrière*'s challenge was spread in all American papers.

Naval strategy could be planned in terms not of fleets, but rather of individual ships meeting at sea and shooting it out, grappled close to one another, until one or the other sank or was captured. A man-of-war was completely on her own. It was up to her commander to seek out an enemy ship of her class and engage her.

News came to Hull that the *Guerrière*, which he had already met off Barnegat Bay, had left the squadron and was cruising about by herself, heading north. He banged his fist on the table and swore that he would find Dacres somewhere at sea and teach him not to cast aspersions on Yankee courage.

On the eighteenth of August, while the *Constitution* was cruising about still trying to pick up the *Guerrière*'s trail, the lookout sang, "Sail ho!"

"Where away?" asked Hull, who had rushed out of his cabin.

"Off the starboard bow, sir!"

"Can you make her out?"

"She's a brig, sir, and she shows no colors."

"Hoist our ensign and make way for her!"

They overhauled the stranger, who suddenly hoisted an American flag and laid to for them. When they came within hailing distance they discovered she was a Boston privateer.

"What news?" Hull asked her captain.

"The *Guerrière*'s cruising close by — we barely got away from her."

"What was her course?"

"Northeast."

"Set the course," Hull ordered, "and we'll try and meet up with her!"

The topmen were sent aloft and every rag of sail was crowded on. Extra lookouts were posted and told to keep a sharp eye peeled. Night passed. The day of August 19 dawned and wore on tensely.

It was late afternoon when Amos, off watch below decks, heard excited shouts and the rush of feet overhead. He ran topside with some other shipmates to find the whole crew crowded at the starboard rail, watching a sliver of white sail skipping far away on the rough, tumbling sea.

"She's a great vessel, sir!" cried the lookout excitedly, peering through the spyglass. "She has tremendous big sails!"

"Make sail for her!" Hull yelled.

She was indeed a great vessel, a man-of-war of their own class. As they approached she shortened sail and waited for them to come up.

The spyglasses showed her to be the *Guerrière*.

As they drew nearer, a sign appeared on one of her topsails: "NOT THE LITTLE BELT!" And her bow deck fired a war signal — a rocket and two signal guns.

"Clear decks for action!" Hull ordered.

The men stampeded over the decks, each knowing his particular task. Officers' bulkheads were taken down and stowed. The ship's carpenters busied themselves making wooden plugs to stop up holes made by enemy cannonballs. The ship's surgeon and his assistants went into the cockpit to prepare for the wounded. Cutlasses were put in racks by the capstan, ready for boarding. Chests of arms were dragged on deck and opened. The decks were sanded, and the sand was scuffed underfoot to prevent men from slipping in blood. And wooden tubs of hot, reeking vinegar were set out on deck, to be used to wash away the smell of blood after the battle was over.

In a few minutes the ship was ready for action. The drums beat to quarters. The men took up their stations — snipers and Marines aloft in the rigging, gunners with their guns loaded and trained on their target, powder monkeys in line — and breathless silence engulfed the ship as they awaited the next order.

The pug-nosed powder boy, Danny Hoagan, was serving Amos's gun. He winked at the men and hitched up his belt, but he was only ten years old and his grin was not quite so cocky as usual. Even Amos, a grown man, felt sober and cold at the thought of what was to happen.

The *Guerrière* opened fire.

Crash! The *Constitution* was hit. A shot fell near the breech of Amos's gun and barely missed exploding it. Long Tom picked up the shot, grinned, and said, "Let's send it back to 'em while it's still hot!"

The gun captain's eyes were fastened on Hull, waiting for the order to fire. But Hull kept silent. The *Guerrière* maneuvered closer and fired again.

Standing stiffly at attention, Amos saw a shell explode

near a port gun, blowing up one of the men and injuring another. Blood stained the scrubbed white boards on the spar deck. Still no order came from Hull to return fire.

Amos wet his lips and stole a look at Bill Fergusson. The Scotchman shrugged and lifted an eyebrow. What was Old Switchell waiting for? Amos's big hands twitched. He felt absurdly exposed there on the spar deck with nothing to do.

The sea was heavy. Both ships were wallowing about, the *Guerrière* trying to come into position to rake them, the *Constitution* managing to avoid her.

Boom! Boom! Boom!

Again the *Guerrière* fired on them.

Crash! The carpenters rushed aft with their wooden plugs. A man fell not far away from Amos and began to crawl along the deck.

Over on the *Guerrière*, Amos could see, a puncheon of molasses was being hoisted up on the mainstay. A crudely lettered sign below it read: "GIVE THE YANKEES SOME SWITCHELL."

Again the lurching seas flung the two vessels close. Suddenly Hull leaped into the air and stamped his foot. "NOW, let 'em have it, boys!" he bellowed.

Instantly every man aboard sprang into action. The powder was fired. The guns went off in unison. The terrific salvo shook the *Constitution* as though she were caught in an earthquake.

When some of the smoke rolled away Amos saw the

damage they had done. The *Guerrière*'s mizzenmast had been shot away! It had fallen over the side, spilling the men in the tops into the sea.

"Huzza, boys!" cried Hull. "Good work! We've made a brig of her! Next time we'll make her a sloop!"

Aboard the *Guerrière* there was frantic bustle. Men under fire were trying to rescue those flung overboard. Carpenters were chopping away at the fallen mast, trying to get the ship clear. A hopelessly snarled tangle of rigging trailed over the stern.

The fallen mast was finally cleared and sank into the sea. The *Guerrière* righted herself and swung back into firing position. Her guns belched smoke and a vengeful iron hail. But the shot went too high, peppering only the *Constitution*'s sails, rigging, and light spars.

The gunners of both ships worked frantically now. Aboard the *Guerrière* the damage was more serious. A stray shot shattered the puncheon of molasses, and the sticky dark fluid oozed along the deck, hindering the movements of the crew.

Then Amos became aware of loud cheers aboard the British frigate. He looked about to see what the enemy had hit. Long Tom pointed aloft. The *Constitution*'s flag had been shot down. It hung low, trailing ingloriously in a tangle of rope from the broken topmast. Amos heard the men on the *Guerrière* shouting, "Huzza! The Yankees have struck their colors! Huzza! Huzza!"

"Struck our colors?" cried Danny Hoagan, who had

just rushed up with a fresh charge from the powder magazine. "Here — catch this!"

He threw the sack of gunpowder at the loader and dashed over to a carpenter who was repairing something nearby. The powder monkey seized a hammer from the sputtering carpenter, scooped up some nails, and before anyone could stop him was clambering up the mast toward the fallen ensign.

He ascended under heavy fire. But the cannonballs and shells flying through the rigging seemed to miss so small and agile a target. The men below cheered. Danny Hoagan reached the torn flag, seized it, and began nailing it firmly to the broken masthead. The smoke of battle curled about him as he worked. The scorched and tattered sails flapped under him. But he seemed as unconcerned as though he were at his usual game of skylarking.

The flag nailed securely, he scrambled down again. The British snipers tried to pick him off, but he got down without even a scratch, a bit pale but still wearing his impudent grin. Breathing hard, he apologized to the angry carpenter who claimed his hammer, and to the officer who came running over to scold him for abandoning his duty. Then he hitched up his belt, winked at the men, and scampered off again about his business.

The enemy gunners were taking better aim now. Several shots struck the *Constitution*'s hull. But so tough were her thick oak sides that one large cannonball bounced off harmlessly into the water. An amazed sailor pointed to the place where it had struck and cried, "I'll be durned, men! Look! Her sides are made of iron! Old Ironsides! Say — huzza for *Old Ironsides*! Huzza!"

The name caught the men's fancy. Overtaken by a wave of affection for their sturdy ship, they passed the new name along, chuckling, liking the sound of it. Soon the whole ship took up the cry: "Huzza! Long live *Old Ironsides*!"

And so amid the thunder of cannon, the smoke of gunpowder, and the raucous cheering of embattled men, the *Constitution* was christened anew.

CHAPTER XI

Home of the Brave

*T*HE CRIPPLED *Guerrière*, hard to manage because of her broken mast, was caught by a huge wave, spun about like a toy ship, and then jammed with her head against the *Constitution*'s stern. Part of her lay over the taffrail. She was now caught in a dangerous position, ready to be raked fore and aft.

The *Constitution*'s stern cannon swept the full length of her, pouring slaughter and confusion on her hapless decks. Men were seen running in panic. The wounded crawled about unattended. Captain Dacres himself was seen desperately trying to maneuver his ship, ordering his men to rally on the foredeck and board the Yankee frigate. And now women appeared on the deck of the *Guerrière*. They crossed the deck under fire, carrying ammunition to the hard-pressed gunners, taking over the job of the powder monkeys.

Many times afterward in his lifetime Amos would

remember that scene: the two ships alone upon the high seas except for a few gulls skimming nearby, grappled close and pouring an infernal cloud of greasy black smoke upon one another while the sun went down behind a rosy bank of clouds.

Now, seizing boarding axe and cutlass, he rushed aft at the order to repel boarders. Several British had leaped into the *Constitution*'s netting and were desperately fighting to get aboard. In a hand-to-hand struggle they were thrust back. High seas then flung the two ships apart again.

Snipers on both ships now shot at the officers, whose uniforms made them conspicuous. The thick hail of musket shots became dreadful. Bill Fergusson had an ear torn off by a musket ball, and Amos was wounded by a ball that lightly grazed his back.

Lieutenant Morris, next in command to Hull, tried to lead them to board the British frigate in a counterattack. The young officer fell, badly wounded, and was carried away pale and unconscious. His place was taken by another officer, who was mortally wounded a few minutes afterward. Lieutenant Morris reappeared, weak and disheveled, the front of his uniform stained with blood, to lead them again in a futile attempt to end the battle by a speedy capture.

On the other ship, Captain Dacres appeared to be wounded as well. Amos saw him stagger and clutch at his shoulder. But he remained at his post, directing his demoralized crew to mount two cannon on the foredeck and sweep the Yankees if they managed to get aboard.

Neither side could board, however, because of the wallowing seas. Bugles blew constantly. Amos rushed from side to side as new alarms sounded. It was sometimes hard to tell which ship the signals came from, so close were they at times.

Then a gun exploded, setting the *Constitution*'s cabin afire. Men rushed to put out the swiftly mounting flames with buckets of brine. That danger removed, Hull ordered his gunners to return to their posts.

The two ships swung clumsily back into firing position. Again the guns thundered at one another, locked almost barrel to barrel. The barrels were so close to the wooden sides that the guns sometimes had to be moved back to be fired.

The *Constitution* drew off and came into firing position once more. Now her gunners had a clear view of their target.

Long Tom rammed the charge down the smooth black bore. "We're gonna make this shot count," he said. "Cut her masts away. We kin do it! Ain't we the crack gunners on this ship?"

Many times during target practice they had hit an empty barrel bobbing about on the sea. For Yankee gunners, this should not be too difficult a target. Amos carefully placed the barrel in position and trained it. Quoin and tackle held it steady while his keen backwoods eyes studied the target — the *Guerrière*'s foremast. He waited for the lurching seas to begin their long roll, and suddenly yelled, "Let 'er rip!"

The powder fizzed. The gun barked, followed by a tremendous rending and crashing like the sound of a giant tree struck by lightning. Leaping away from the dangerous recoil, Amos caught his foot in some loose tackle. He was flung flat on his face and half-stunned by the impact. As he lay there he felt rather than saw some heavy dark object flying over his head.

The next moment he jumped up, unhurt. Everyone about him was cheering wildly. After the smoke rolled away they saw that they had hit their target! The *Guerrière*'s foremast had broken in two. Falling, it had struck the mainmast which was also tottering. The crew was awed to see the third and last mast also go down, tearing and thundering to the deck.

Amos could not wrench his eyes from the sight of the stricken ship, now tossing helplessly, utterly at the mercy of the heavy seas. Her gun ports rolled uselessly under water. Her guns were silenced. An hour ago a proud and stately ship, she was now nothing but a derelict hulk.

He felt a twinge of pity for her, but then fierce jubilation swept him as he realized that the battle was over and won. Everyone aboard the *Constitution* was wild with joy. Even Hull danced up and down and yelled, "Brave lads! Good lads! She's ours now!"

On the stricken ship, sailors hauled down the Cross

Constitution and *Guerrière*, after Francoise Roux. (Private collection; courtesy Peabody Museum of Salem)

of St. George and hoisted the white flag of surrender on the broken mast. At the same moment the ship dropped suddenly to leeward and fired a distress signal.

The crew embraced one another with tears, and then Amos noticed Long Tom. The giant sailor was sitting on the deck, propped against a huge wooden tub. He breathed painfully. His eyes rolled in distress. His lips were working, but they made no sound. As they all rushed to him and bent over him, they saw that he was mortally wounded. A flying piece of shrapnel had hit him in the side.

Why, it was meant for me! thought Amos dazedly, remembering the moment when his foot had caught in the gun tackle. He knelt and lifted Long Tom. On his back he bore the dying sailor to sickbay to see whether anything could be done for him.

Amos stayed with Long Tom. Moses Smith and Bill Fergusson came in too, and other men from Long Tom's crew.

"Captain Dacres has just come aboard and surrendered his sword to Old Switchell," Fergusson whispered, his head bandaged with bloody linen. "He's fair wounded, too."

Long Tom's dimming eyes seemed to focus just once. He tried feebly to raise himself, hearing the jubilant sound of cheering and singing. "Listen," he whispered. "What — ?"

"The enemy struck his colors," Amos told him.

Long Tom lay back. His grayish lips moved. Amos had to bend very close to hear what the sailor was trying to say.

"Struck . . . colors. Huzza. Huzz —" His feeble voice trailed off.

They turned away and left him.

Back on deck Amos found the pungent smell of hot vinegar everywhere. The decks had been washed down. Here and there places were being scrubbed to remove stains. He heard the busy hum of saws and the quite cheerful sound of hammering as the carpenters got to work repairing the main damage. Sailmakers were mending the torn sails. The grog tub had been brought on deck, and men with the grime and sweat of battle still on them crowded about for a victory toast.

"Brace up, laddie," said Bill Fergusson, gripping Amos by his hard young shoulder. "There's naught we can do now for the poor fellow."

"Here come the prisoners," said Moses Smith. "Poor devils, they suffered much more than we."

Pale and proud, his arm bandaged in clean white linen, Captain Dacres stood chatting with Captain Hull amidships, where the prisoners were being brought aboard. A file of weary, grimy men paraded past them. Dacres seemed moved to see his beaten men. The British officers, some of whom were openly weeping, were relieved of their swords and sent to the cabin. The sailors were sent below and put in irons. As they filed wearily down the hatchway, one of the filthy British prisoners called out to the men at the grog tub: "'Ere, Yankees — give us a swig of that stuff! We could fair use it!"

The wounded prisoners were removed to sickbay and made as comfortable as conditions permitted. There were many wounded. Some were beyond help. The usually clean and spotless hospital, with its operating chair, white porcelain washbasins and round bathtub, and rows of snowy hammocks, was now a shambles of soiled and blood-soaked linen. Captain Hull went from hammock to hammock with a word of comfort for each of the wounded, both his own men and those who had been enemies but a short while before.

The whole battle had lasted not more than an hour.

The *Constitution*'s losses were light, after all — only seven dead and seven wounded. Aboard the *Guerrière*, there were heavy casualties — fifteen killed, eight missing and sixty-three wounded.

The *Guerrière* was sinking; six feet of water had risen in her hold. But on *Old Ironsides* all was practically shipshape again in a short while. The frigate had suffered the loss of her figurehead — King Neptune astride a dolphin, a memento of the war with Tripoli. Her steering gear was shattered, and the wheel was removed from the *Guerrière* to replace it. But though she had been engaged at close range, her hull had not suffered one vital shot. The holes she had between wind and water were easily repaired by carpenters' plugs.

"Ain't she a lucky ship, though?" a sailor asked. "*Old Ironsides*. I bet the name will stick to her 'til doomsday, so long as a chip of her's left afloat. Not a mast lost. Nothing a few nails can't make tight an' tidy again."

But the *Guerrière* was in a bad way. Men were put aboard to pump out her hold. She continued to fill, so everyone was evacuated. Somehow she remained floating through the night. But in the morning, since she was beyond any hope of salvage as a prize, Hull decided to blow her up.

After the *Constitution* had sailed three miles off, she hove to and her crew waited for the *Guerrière*'s end. She sank before their eyes in a crescendo of crashes and lightning flares, all her guns firing a last salute. The

Americans saw her hull snap asunder in the middle, flinging her quarter-deck high into the air. A heavy cloud hovered over the place where she went under.

Captain Dacres, standing beside Hull, handed back the spyglass. He turned, and with lowered head walked slowly to his quarters.

Old Ironsides put into Boston with the Cross of St. George trailing below the Stars and Stripes. For two days she anchored off Long Wharf, sprucing up, while crowds jammed the docks to have a look at her and to cheer her victory.

She had come home in a dark hour. The war was going badly. On land, defeat had followed defeat, and the people were discouraged. Only two weeks before, Detroit had surrendered her large garrison to the British. Fort Dearborn (later Chicago) was practically razed to the ground. The Great Lakes were completely in the hands of the enemy.

Old Ironsides' victory meant a turning point in the fortunes of the war. When Hull set foot ashore and delivered his prisoners, parading them up State Street, the cannons of shore and harbor roared salute after salute. The people of Boston danced in the streets. Bands played everywhere. Church bells pealed joyously. Taphouses gave free ale. Women leaned out of windows to throw garlands about the heroes from the *Constitution*.

In Faneuil Hall there was a great banquet for Hull and his heroes, with six hundred plates set. Even Danny

Constitution moored in Boston Harbor with a contingent of the Boston Light Infantry marching in foreground. Lithograph by Fitz Hugh Lane. (Boston Athenaeum)

Hoagan came in for his share of glory. The little powder monkey was petted and made much of by the ladies. A gentleman presented him with a silver snuffbox, for which he had as much use as a squirrel has for three tails.

Nor did Hull forget Long Tom. When a gentleman, offended at the sight of white and black sailors singing arm-in-arm through the streets, asked Hull how he had managed to win such a brilliant victory with so many black men in his crew, Old Switchell replied with spirit that he had never had any better fighters than his black sailors — that they had stripped to the waist and fought like demons with a courage that seemed utterly insensible to danger.

All over the land traveled the news that a great victory

had been won by the little navy. Reports reached England, where furious attacks appeared in some of the newspapers. "Are we to be beaten by a bunch of pine boards under a bit of striped bunting?" asked one sarcastically. From that time onward, the British called the American navy "fir frigates."

But the United States won the war, as everyone knows, and out of the turmoil came a national anthem: new words written to the tune of an old English drinking song.

No, the *Constitution* was not merely pine boards and bunting. It was the home of the brave: a parcel of green bushwhackers, plain and simple Yankees like Amos Brown, Long Tom, Bill Fergusson, Moses Smith.

Part Three

CHAPTER XII

Saved by a Poet

*B*Y THE YEAR 1828, every schoolchild in the land knew all about the famous battles of *Old Ironsides*. Her picture hung in almost every front parlor. Even in lonely log cabins on the frontier, deep in the woods, far from any ocean, backwoodsmen pored over her neat lines, counted her guns and her sails, and puzzled over her complicated ropes and rigging.

For those who had served aboard her she was truly a lucky ship. She had bravely withstood storms, fire, cannon. Her masts had never fallen, and she had never lost a battle.

Yet the historic frigate was due to die.

Time had conquered her proud deck. Warped beams and rotting planks made her no longer seaworthy; it was dangerous to take her to sea again. The forces of rust and decay, at work for more than thirty years, were accomplishing what no enemy had been able to do. Shabby old derelict — it didn't even pay to scrape the barnacles off her, or to give her a new suit of sails.

She had just made what appeared to be her last sea voyage, convoying the relief ships sent by the people of America to the embattled people of Greece, who were struggling to end more than 350 years of Ottoman rule. Now, after her return, she was laid up and officially condemned to be scrapped. Her days of usefulness were over now. She was fit for nothing but junk.

Old Ironsides might never have sailed again, but a poet came to her rescue.

In 1830 a young law student named Oliver Wendell Holmes happened to pick up a copy of a Boston paper and read that the secretary of the navy had ordered the historic old frigate *Constitution* to be demolished and sold for junk. Indignation ran through him as he read.

Somehow the ship seemed very much alive — a famous personage, really — and the thought of her being condemned in her old age was more than Holmes could bear. Why, she was beautiful — the proudest, swiftest thing that ever sailed! Better to give her a Viking's death, to crowd on all her ragged sail and send her out into the storm, than to sell her for worthless junk!

So deep were Holmes's feelings that he dashed them off in the form of a poem on the back of an old envelope. This is what he wrote:

Ay, tear her tattered ensign down!
  Long has it waved on high,
And many an eye has danced to see
  That banner in the sky;
Beneath it rung the battle shout,
  And burst the cannon's roar; —
The meteor of the ocean air
  Shall sweep the clouds no more.

Her deck, once red with heroes' blood,
  Where knelt the vanquished foe,
When winds were hurrying o'er the flood,
  And waves were white below,
No more shall feel the victor's tread,
  Or know the conquered knee; —
The harpies of the shore shall pluck
  The eagle of the sea!

Oh, better that her shattered hulk
  Should sink beneath the wave;
Her thunders shook the mighty deep,
  And there should be her grave;
Nail to the mast her holy flag,
  Set every threadbare sail,
And give her to the god of storms,
  The lightning and the gale!

Without showing it to anyone, he hurriedly sent the poem off to the newspaper and signed it with a modest initial, "H." The poem appeared, and it caught the public's imagination immediately. At Dane Law School,

Holmes was surprised to hear his work being quoted by one of the professors. He finally admitted to his classmates that he was the author of the poem everyone was quoting.

Requests came in from other newspapers for permission to reprint. More and more newspapers copied the verses. People clipped the poem out and carried it around in their pockets. Schoolteachers read it to their classes. Orators recited it. As sentiment gathered, people wrote indignant letters to Congress to save the historic old ship.

Finally Congress heeded. It voted a sum of money for the repair of *Old Ironsides.*

She was overhauled from stem to stern and from topmast to keel, and was recommissioned. With a new coat of paint and a new set of sails she put to sea again under one of her old commanders — Isaac Hull, Old Switchell, of the time of her glory.

The days that lay ahead of her now were peaceful. Her days of battle were over and gone. But she was still to sail many thousands of miles and to have many adventures yet.

And thus, thanks to a poet, even time did not conquer her after all.

CHAPTER XIII

Mad Jack and the Mandarins

*I*T WAS a blue Monday.

Old Jack, the captain, was suffering twinges of gout. He appeared on deck, a patriarchal figure with flowing white hair, leaning heavily on his black whalebone cane. When Skipper Jack Percival carried his cane, his crew knew that it meant "look out for squalls ahead." His gout was extra bad, and he would be extra hard on the men.

He limped slowly toward the mast where the crew was assembled, looked them over with eyes as blue and cold as the sea, and began reading the list of crimes for the past week: "Seaman Mike Loughlin — twelve lashes with the colt for skulking on watch! Seaman Potts — eight for untidy appearance! Seaman Pollock — ten for washing clothes without permission! Seaman Grimes — fifteen for sleeping on watch! Seaman Zimmerman —

twelve for skulking!" He went on and on down a list that seemed interminable.

As his name was called, each sailor stepped forward, took off his shirt, allowed himself to be seized up at the grating, and manfully took the brutal punishment. The boatswain, seeing that the Old Man's back was turned, tried to go as lightly as possible. Each sailor went away muttering something under his breath — some epithet not too complimentary to the tall, straight, white-haired old captain, known among his crew as Mad Jack, Jack the old seadog, and Jack the crazy curmudgeon.

Last on the list was an old sailor, grizzled of hair, gentle of manner, usually faithful and obedient. Every man wondered now what he could possibly have done to stir up the skipper's bile.

The old sailor took off his cap, fixed his eyes mournfully on the captain's impassive face, and waited for the axe to fall.

"Mark you now," said Captain Jack to his men, "I never overlook good conduct or bad! I promote this man to coxswain, for he has been a good and faithful seaman, rarely surpassed, and never skulking when an order is given!"

A radiant smile lit up the sailor's face.

The men nudged one another. That was Old Jack for you! Old Jack with his gout, his bile, his tantrums, his unexpected kindnesses. As fine a captain as anyone in the world, except that he was so strict with his men and read them the articles of war three times on Sundays and twice on Tuesdays.

Mad Jack Percival was skipper of *Old Ironsides* in 1844. The historic old ship, her days of battle forever ended, was now off on a scientific expedition. She was to circumnavigate the globe, taking two and a half years for the project. Her course lay round the tip of Africa to Zanzibar, the Indian Ocean, the China seas, the South Sea islands, and home again by Cape Horn — a delightful adventure cruise, one that would gather valuable information about the far corners of the earth.

At Rio de Janeiro the ship took aboard a famous naturalist, a Philadelphian. Dr. J. C. Reinhardt had been hired by the government to collect specimens of plants, seeds, minerals, birds, and insects for the Scientific Institute at Washington. The doctor, whom the men called "that bug-hunter" and "Quaker Doc," had been busy with an expedition up the Amazon River when Captain Jack picked him up.

Captain Percival also had orders to explore minutely and to chart the coasts of Sumatra and Borneo. For more than fifty years Yankee merchantmen had been visiting these waters, which were as yet very imperfectly charted. Such mariners' charts as existed could not be trusted. Islands appeared in the wrong places. Hidden rocks, shoals, and reefs were not indicated. Traders traveled here at great risk, for the shores were inhabited by wild aborigines or fierce and hostile Malays, and shipwreck on these coasts often meant death.

In addition, Old Jack had a little business on the side: a matter of trade rivalry with the British in Borneo, and a matter to take up with the rajah of Sumatra, whose pirates were molesting peaceful Yankee merchantmen.

The ship set out from Rio de Janeiro in holiday dress. Instead of her familiar black hull and white gun-deck stripe, she was now a light, cool gray with a red ribbon about her middle. Captain Jack had his men repaint the ship, thinking the light color would make the ship cooler. Since most of their long voyage would lie in the tropics, he was naturally concerned for the health of his crew.

Leaving Rio, they rounded the Cape of Good Hope where they failed to meet with the Flying Dutchman, then to the famed Spice Islands.

At Sumatra they stopped at a notorious pirates' nest. On this wild and treacherous coast the entire crew of a Yankee merchantman had been slaughtered only a short time before. The savage Malays still had a yen for ambushing and kidnaping Yankee captains. Old Jack, almost too ill to walk, limped ashore with his black whalebone cane, carrying a letter from the President of the United States to the rajah of Sumatra. He added a little postscript of his own: he would personally come back and blow the whole place to kingdom come — royal palace, monkeys, tigers, and all — if ever again any trader was molested on these shores.

The rajah's reply was that he wanted only peace and commerce with the rajah of the United States of America. He would personally cut off the head of any of his subjects who interfered hereafter with the pepper trade. That little matter settled, Old Jack went back to his cabin to nurse his gout, and the ship pursued its scientific explorations.

A wild, uncharted coast. Soundings taken every minute. Very slow progress sailing and maneuvering between the rocks and shoals. The sailing was intricate, requiring expert seamanship and constant attention.

All night long tom-toms throbbed in the dark jungles. Watch fires, the natives' defense against prowling tigers, burned. By day, the tar between the deck planks broiled and bubbled in the sultry heat.

Dr. Reinhardt seemed not to mind the tigers and other fierce creatures that prowled the jungles. He went ashore with his butterfly net, bottles, and other paraphernalia, snagging insects and happily filling his pockets with chunks of worthless-looking rock. He seemed not to mind the mosquitoes or the sultry, bone-sapping heat.

But the men succumbed. Day after day the sick report worsened. Dysentery swept through the ship. Old Jack himself was not immune. He was laid low in his cabin while the lieutenant took over the ship. Then a few cases

of yellow fever appeared among the crew. Old Jack began
to fear in earnest for the health of his men.

Once long ago, when he was still a young man, the
captain had been on a plague ship. Off the West Indies,
the whole crew had come down with the terrible yellow
jack — a plague not then understood, which was thought
to be caused by the "miasmatic vapors" of certain damp
tropical places. The entire crew had died, every last man
aboard except Old Jack himself — who was young Jack
then — and the ship's dog, a huge animal with a shaggy
coat.

Dysentery was bad enough. But there was nothing
sailors dreaded more than an epidemic of yellow fever.
There were several deaths this time, and gloom settled
over the ship. The men went about their tasks hollow-
eyed, as if clothed in lead. Many who were stricken but
not too ill to lend a hand to the overworked crew looked
as if the flesh were slowly melting from their bones. The
ship lost its trim and tidy appearance. The rigging was
slack, the sails hung loose, and men were seated about
the decks in attitudes of weariness or despair.

Old Jack ranted and raved at the ship's surgeon, as if
he were to blame for the ship's being "a floating pest-
house." The surgeon angrily maintained that only the
bad food and water were to blame. The yellow fever
would clear up when they put out to sea. The dysentery would clear up when they reached Singapore, where
the crew could get fresh food and water.

The work of soundings finally completed, the ship headed for Singapore. Calms delayed them. By the time they made port, half the crew was ill. Looking battered, her gray hull streaked with blotches of rust and barnacles, *Old Ironsides* was actually nothing more nor less than a hospital ship.

Other ships sent aid as soon as her disabled crew could manage to make her fast. But just as the ship's surgeon had said, fresh food, fresh water, and rest from the steaming jungle heat worked wonders from the first day on. Old Jack took plenty of time, staying on to clean his ship and make sure everything was shipshape once again before he put out to sea.

One day he came bustling aboard in a great rush to be off. He had learned that a British steamer had just left Singapore headed for Borneo. She had an agent aboard who was empowered to sign a trade treaty with the sultan. Old Jack had similar business with the sultan. He must get there first and head the British off!

The clumsy steamers of those days, with their wooden paddle wheels, were just beginning to compete with the old wooden sailing ships. Captain Jack, who looked down on steamships, thought he could race the steamer and beat it to Borneo.

But he ran into calms again. When the frigate put in at Borneo, Captain Jack learned he was just three days too late. The steamer had come and gone. The sultan had signed all rights away to the British, and he and his people were now subjects of the king of England. The Americans were too late to do any dickering for the products of the island's rich gold mines and for other minerals.

So Captain Jack resumed his scientific work. The slow task of taking minute bearings and soundings went on.

Doc Reinhardt disappeared in a small boat up one of the wild jungle rivers. He had just two sailors with him, armed only with revolvers. When they failed to return at night, everyone was certain they had met with some foul play.

Anxious hours ticked away. Next morning, a second boat went after the first. Everyone breathed more easily when, late in the afternoon, the search party returned with the naturalist and the two sailors in tow. They had gone several miles upriver, the indefatigable doctor lured on and on by strange plants unknown in America. They had spent the night in a remote village of headhunters with filed teeth.

Quaker Doc had traded practically everything the expedition had, except the revolvers, for a beautiful specimen of a smoked, dried, and shrunken human head. He was as happy as a small boy with a new set of marbles at his rare find, though Mike Loughlin, one of the lost sailors, remarked disgustedly, "It's a miracle indeed we're here to tell the tale of it, what with poisonous snakes and all, and heathens who'd as soon eat a man as shake hands with him!"

But Quaker Doc laughed and made light of the whole thing. The quiet, spectacled naturalist, small and spare, rose several notches in the eyes of the crew. He was absolutely fearless in the pursuit of his everlasting dried bugs, stuffed bird carcasses, and pressed leaves.

Old Jack's peppery spirits had returned. The crew hopped about lively, the ship humming with activity. Now that their health was good, they dropped anchor at Cochin China in quite a different condition from when they had limped into Singapore.

A Chinese junk, clumsy as a scow, came to meet them. She was gaily decorated with little flags, red-painted cannon, and a crew all in red. Two huge painted eyes on the prow of the ship were supposed to make her see her way through the water. But in spite of this curious custom, the Chinese junks were notoriously awkward in the water. The wall-sided thing almost wrecked itself before her chattering crew managed to bring her alongside. Then, with stately pomp, three mandarins and an interpreter came aboard the frigate.

The mandarins were port authorities, representatives of the king of Cochin China, who dwelt in the Celestial City where foreigners could not enter. They had long black pigtails that reached below their waists, and wore rich blue coats of silk and brocade and little skullcaps topped by a gold button and two peacock feathers. They were "two-feather mandarins" — mandarins of the middle rank.

Gravely they inspected the ship, being shown about *Old Ironsides* by the lieutenant. The interpreter, a poor scholar who was not of the mandarin class, had a vocabulary of about fifty English words. But he made up in smiles and bows for what he lacked in subtleties of language.

Sometime during the proceedings, he managed to slip away and hand Old Jack a sealed letter. Then, evidently fearful of what he had just done, he turned pale.

"Please!" he said. "Secret letter! No talk!"

He put his fingers to his lips and, pointing to the letter, whisked away.

Captain Jack looked at the envelope. It was addressed to the admiral of the French fleet. He broke the seals and read. It was in French, a language with which he had become acquainted during his years of knocking about the sea. The contents made his eyes pop.

"I am condemned to death without delay. Hasten, or all is finished!" the letter ended. And it was signed, "Dominique Lefevre, Bishop of Cochin China."

The bishop, who was a French subject, had been seized, jailed, and condemned to death by the king for carrying on missionary work. Several of his Chinese converts were also in jail, wearing iron collars about their necks. The little village in which he had lived and worked had been burned, and the church pillaged and destroyed.

Captain Jack knew that he could not go looking for

the French admiral. The worthy bishop would be put to death before help could come. He decided then and there that he would free the bishop himself. So he had the three mandarins seized and locked in the brig. He explained to them that he was holding them as hostages for the bishop's life. The interpreter was sent ashore with a strongly worded letter to the king: if anything happened to the bishop, something would certainly happen to the king's mandarins. The one thing that bothered Old Jack was that they were only two-feather mandarins. Maybe the king of Cochin China did not value the lives of two-feather mandarins too highly.

The frigate's crew was greatly excited. Nobody knew how far Mad Jack might go, for he had a will of iron; the more he was opposed, the more grimly he hung on. It was a crazy adventure, and might well end in shooting. The frigate moved in closer and trained her guns on the Chinese fort.

Of course Captain Jack Percival had no business risking an act of war for a French national. But, he fumed, pounding the deck with his whalebone cane, "He's a countryman of Lafayette's, ding-busted-burn-it, and a bishop to boot!"

Jittery days ticked off. At last a message came from the king. His minister was waiting for Old Jack ashore, ready to straighten matters out. Captain Percival was directed to bring the hostages with him.

The Old Man stuffed himself into his full-dress uniform — a frightful punishment in that sultry climate — picked an armed bodyguard, and took his prisoners ashore. There, as he had feared, he met treachery. No king's minister was waiting. The whole party was ambushed, and while no one was harmed, the hostages were seized and taken away.

Fuming, Old Jack returned to his ship. Now he had no hostages, and the king of Cochin China must be laughing up his wide silken sleeve. The next move was up to Captain Jack.

The Old Man decided there was only one way to get to the king: to march right into his palace and demand an audience. So he went ashore again, this time with three boatloads of armed sailors, and marched up to the Celestial City.

Outside the walls he was met by a frightened deputation of three-feather mandarins — those of the topmost rank, sacred even to the king. These high dignitaries begged Old Jack not to profane the Celestial City by setting his barbaric foot inside the walls, or they would lose their venerable heads. Old Jack halted and called for the king's minister. If that worthy did not appear immediately, ready to dicker with him, then he and his sailors would march directly through the gates and start profaning right and left. The king and his whole court would have to abandon the place as if a plague had struck it.

A mandarin so splendid that he had eight bearers to

carry his jeweled sedan chair came to give them an audience. With him was the court interpreter — the same poor scholar who had handed Captain Jack the bishop's letter.

The mandarin haughtily cooled himself with a peacock feather fan while Old Jack stood up in his fighting clothes, leaning on his cane, and delivered a lengthy ultimatum. The translator passed it on to the mandarin, boiling it down to about half-a-dozen words. Old Jack waited. The mandarin gravely sent for a silken scroll and dictated a long reply. He handed the interpreter the scroll, who took it and, fixing his onyx eyes on Captain Jack, rendered it as follows: "No bishop here! All lies! Go back home!"

Then the mandarin bowed gravely, got into his jeweled sedan, and went back into the Celestial City.

Old Jack let him go. What was the captain to do now? There was only one thing left: to go back to the ship, get the entire crew, march on the jail, tear it down, and carry off the bishop by force. If it meant risking his commission, or even war, well then. He had gone too far now to stop.

But on the beach sat a man in a cassock. When he saw the party of sailors trudging toward the *Constitution* he jumped up, rushed to Old Jack, seized his wrinkled hand, and cried in French, "Oh, sir! You saved my life! They set me free just an hour ago!"

The bishop of Cochin China sailed aboard *Old Iron-*

sides as the captain's guest. Not much later the Americans handed him over to a French warship. The crew had many a chuckle over Mad Jack's escapade with the king of Cochin China.

Mad Jack Percival, for all his faults, was a good captain — brave, resourceful, and not without sudden kindnesses to his men. He brought *Old Ironsides* safely to port after circumnavigating the globe in two years, five months, and seventeen days. On this cruise *Old Ironsides* sailed almost 55,000 miles and visited twenty-five foreign ports. Twenty-seven of her crew died on the way.

Dr. Reinhardt's collection consisted of the following:

4 boxes of geological specimens
3 boxes of dried specimens of plants
1 box of dried specimens of plants and seeds
3 boxes of birds

Not all of it went to dusty museums. Some of the seeds of plants hitherto unknown in this country were used for experimentation. As for the doctor, the little, spectacled man left the ship at Rio de Janeiro and went back up the Amazon again.

Captain Jack Percival, like the other sea captains of his day, believed a crew should be whipped well to keep up its morale. His men were frequently punished for skulking — that is, for not jumping fast enough to obey an order.

Captain John Percival (Mad Jack). Portrait by Chester Harding. (Peabody Museum of Salem)

But Old Jack's type was soon to vanish from the sea. The custom of flogging, which surely dated back to the days when galley slaves were lashed by their overseers, was arousing public sentiment. Not long after *Old Ironsides'* voyage, in 1850, flogging of seamen was abolished by act of Congress.

Already there were new advances in shipbuilding. Changes were taking place that would make ships independent of wind and weather. Wooden ships were giving way to ships of iron and steel. Sail and wind power, which had served seafarers for centuries, was now giving way to the power of steam.

CHAPTER XIV

Black Market in Ebony

*B*OTTLE OF BEER, the African pilot, stood beside the helm. Occasionally he scanned the sky, lifted his face to the wind, and sniffed. The tall sailor's uniform included a necklace of powerful *gris-gris*, or magic charms, and a battered old straw hat.

He was a *krooman*. That was what the native African pilots were called. The kroomen were well known to Yankee whalers and merchantmen touching at the coast of Africa, and were highly respected. Bottle of Beer had been hired to help pilot the *Constitution* along the African coast during her 1853 patrol in search of slave ships.

He was a stalwart, dignified man, athletic in build, and he spoke the languages of several tribes, which made him a useful interpreter. Long ago some sailor had given him his whimsical name, and it had stuck for good. The kroomen all bore names such as Ginger Pop, Black Pep-

once struck some Yankee sailor's fancy.

Bottle of Beer, of course, had his African name, which the sailors found difficult to pronounce. If his nickname seemed odd to him, he gave no sign. He, too, had his own nicknames for some of the sailors. They did not know this, for he kept them to himself.

Bottle of Beer wrinkled his nostrils. He pointed upwind. "Slave ship somewhere there," he announced matter-of-factly.

"Think so?" said the lieutenant. He took his glasses and swept the ocean. "I don't see a thing," he said.

"Oh, she be there all right," the tall krooman insisted. "I can smell her. She is a bad ship. Plenty of sick aboard."

"Danged if I don't think he's right!" said the helmsman, also wrinkling his nose. "I just got a whiff of something — something poisonous enough to be a slaver!"

The curious taint could soon be detected by all. Veteran sailors of the African squadron could recognize it. If wind and weather were just right, the odor of a slave ship could carry as far as five miles downwind. This meant a terribly overcrowded ship, one that had perhaps experienced storms, on which half the slaves were already ill or dying.

Pretty soon the *Constitution*'s crew saw the slave ship beating toward them down the wind. They could tell at once she was a slaver, even though the wind shifted and the sinister odor disappeared, because, recognizing *Old Ironsides* by her lofty sails even at that great distance, the stranger had instantly put about and tried to make a run for it.

The commodore came on deck and studied her through the glasses. She was a clipper ship — a fast sailer. The slave ships were always of the clipper or schooner class, for the slave traffic was illegal and they depended on making a quick getaway. It was soon apparent that the frigate could not overtake her. The *Constitution* hung on as long as she could, but despite everything the slave smugglers got away.

Old Ironsides altered course and put about. Commodore Isaac Mayo sighed and returned to his cabin. It was an old story, repeated over and over again.

Old Ironsides had been given an assignment for which she was not suited. For months she had conscientiously patrolled the waters of the slave coast, on watch for slavers, and chased every suspicious vessel she sighted. Yet her journey had been fruitless. Not a single capture had she made. Not a single slaver had she overhauled.

America had outlawed the importation of slaves in 1807 and declared it an act of piracy in 1820. Still, everyone knew that the smuggling of vast numbers of slaves into the southern states flourished unchecked. The lot of slaves in America was so hard that they were dying off faster than new ones could be born. The great demand for them insured sizable profits in smuggling fresh slaves into the country.

Up and down the west coast of Africa, in canebrakes and forests and by jungle rivers, barracoons were hidden. These were places of terror: huge stockades, or jungle concentration camps, where kidnapped men, women, and children were held awaiting the white man's slave ships. The African slave trade was very old and very profitable and would be a long time in dying out.

Everyone knew that the slave traders, who winked at the law, had their spies and lookouts all along the coast. These spies knew the movements of every warship in those waters. The towering frigate with her lofty sails was easy to spot a long way off. Slave ships could usually sight her before she could see them. And as they were always fast ships which depended upon their heels, they could always manage to get away from the more cumbersome frigate even if she did give chase.

What was most maddening to the commodore was the abuse of the American flag. Under a joint treaty with America, England also policed the African coast. The British kept a large patrol of warships, both sailing and steam vessels, in those waters, and a slave smuggler was always in great danger of running into a British man-of-war and being captured. But — and here was the rub — no British ship could board or search any vessel flying the American flag. Shady ships of every nation engaged in the nefarious smuggling of slaves carried a spare American flag to run up just in case they ran into a British patrol!

The American squadron consisted of just three ships, *Old Ironsides* and two small brigs. *Old Ironsides* thus had to patrol the enormous stretch of coastline single-handedly, and every slaver within miles knew exactly where she was and whither she was bound. The slavers seemingly had little to fear from the Yankee "squadron." A captain had only to run up the American flag and go his way in peace. Thus the flag was being abused and defiled, used simply as a cover for the smuggling of slaves.

By every sign the slave trade, far from being suppressed, was actually on the increase. British cruisers brought news of cargoes of slaves carried off right under their noses, of ships whose captains defied them with double sets of papers and flags. It was an infuriating situation.

Old Ironsides had now reached the halfway point of her long cruise: the Congo. The Congo River was studded with wild, uncharted islands grown over with savage jungle. Hyenas howled on its shores, lions stalked the canebrakes, and elephant herds trumpeted in the forests.

The Congo region was an especially notorious haunt of slave smugglers. Hidden islands isolated by swift and treacherous currents held barracoons. Slaves were passed downriver from island to island in the dead of night. Raiding parties stalked the villages. No one in this region was safe from kidnaping. The Congo was noted for the vast numbers of slaves it had furnished to America.

One hot, steaming morning just about at daybreak, the frigate's lookout sighted a sail. The ship was several miles out to sea, far from sight of land, yet the muddy stain of the ocean told the crew that they were still in the region of Africa's mightiest river. The other ship had come up rather close to them in the night. Now it seemed the sudden discovery of the frigate threw her into a panic. Immediately she put about and took to her heels, going through all the usual antics of a suspicious vessel. The commodore set the course in pursuit.

His quarry was a schooner. She had been heading toward land, but now put out to sea in the hopes of giving *Old Ironsides* the slip. But she had come too near to get away easily. The frigate hung on, and even outmaneuvered her. For every trick the runaway knew, the commodore knew two more.

The Americans could not make out her nationality. She had hauled down her colors and was sailing without a flag.

"She's waiting for us to show our colors first," growled the commodore. "Then the scalawag will try to doublecross us! Run up a British flag at our masthead and fire a gun at her. Let's see what her answer will be!"

The English flag was hoisted aboard *Old Ironsides*, and a gun ordering the schooner to show her colors was fired. The schooner ran up the Stars and Stripes!

"So she's a Yankee, damn her!" the commodore said. "*Now* run up our true colors, and fire another gun!"

When the schooner saw that she was being pursued by an American warship she became more desperate. To make her ballast lighter and her speed faster, her crew cast overboard almost everything movable — a couple of cannon that had been hidden on her deck, some heavy spars, boxes, ammunition, and finally even all of her small boats. That did not help her. She was finally overhauled and brought into the lee of the frigate. That meant she was cut off from the wind and now had no avenue of escape.

The guns ordered her to lay to. Seeing that all was up, her captain could do nothing but obey. The schooner's crew hauled down her sails and waited to be boarded.

Commodore Mayo picked some armed sailors and went aboard her. They met no resistance. There was nothing suspicious in sight. The schooner's crew, a score or so of sullen-looking roughnecks, glowered at their captors but allowed themselves to be disarmed and taken prisoner.

The captain came forward. He was a hard-featured, truculent fellow who angrily demanded an explanation for the "outrage" on his vessel. His ship, the *H. N. Gambrill*, out of New York, was an honest merchantman trading in palm oil.

"Honest merchantmen don't run from the law," said the commodore. "Your true trade is ebony, isn't it?"

Ebony was the code name smugglers used for a cargo of slaves.

"There isn't a single slave aboard!" sneered the schooner's captain. "You don't have a shred of evidence. For all your highhandedness, you'll have to release my crew and let me proceed about my business!"

The commodore shrugged, demanded the ship's papers, and ordered a search of the vessel.

It was true that without evidence they would have to let the schooner go on her way unmolested, no matter how shady her antics, no matter how strong the suspicion that she was actually a slaver. Some captains of slavers had been known to throw their human cargo overboard when pursued at sea — letting the Africans drown or be killed by sharks, just so no evidence would be found when the law boarded them!

The lieutenant raised the hatches and had a look at the schooner's hold. It was true: there were no slaves below. But the schooner had not run from the law for nothing. She *was* a slaver, all right.

Down in the dark maw of the ship where cargo was usually stowed, all was in readiness for a large shipment of slaves. The crew had laid a "slave deck," rough, unplaned planks placed carefully together over the tops of barrels to make a temporary platform or deck. The space between this crude deck and the ceiling of the hold was only two feet high. In this coffinlike space the miserable victims would be stashed like cargo. Every inch of space was precious; it meant another slave, profits in the slave markets. So every inch would be used.

On such a slave deck the victims could not even sit up. They would make the perilous crossing lying on their sides, breast to back, spoon fashion, shackled to one another and unable even to turn. In bad weather the hatches would be closed tight. Those who did not die of illness, starvation, or grief would die from lack of air.

Such slave decks were laid only on the eve of taking the slaves aboard. The *Gambrill* had been ready to load. *Old Ironsides* had actually intercepted her while she was on her way to a barracoon.

There were other signs, too, of her sinister trade. The barrels under the slave deck held thousands of gallons of water and enough coarse and tainted food for an army. In a locked compartment was an enormous copper cauldron set in bricks, the kind used on slavers to stew up a mess for the captives. It had just been installed. The cement between the bricks was still wet.

A checkup of the crew showed three men who were not accounted for. Two were mean-eyed, slovenly roughnecks; the third, a fastidious Spanish gentleman, a man seemingly of some education. The three claimed to be passengers who were destitute and were working their way to America. But a search of their belongings turned up several thousand dollars in American gold dollars. Undoubtedly the shady "passengers" were the slave dealers, who had come aboard to clinch the transaction and supervise the loading. Still, there was nothing to prove this.

Commodore Mayo confronted the captain again. "This ship is a slaver. Under the law, I am confiscating it and relieving you of its command."

"You'll pay for this outrage!" stormed the captain. "Because you've not enough evidence, and you know it, to hold good in a court of law!"

The commodore shrugged. "I'll chance it. As for your passengers, they are free to go. It's true I've no shred of evidence against them. The rest of you come aboard the frigate with me."

"Sir, if you let those three murderous, thieving, triple-dyed skunks go free, you're making a big mistake! They're part of a big gang of slavers operating on this coast."

The man who came forward to make this statement was one of the schooner's crew. He seemed a dour, sullen individual much like the rest, and had been eyeing all the proceedings with the other prisoners under guard.

"I'm the ship's cook," he continued, glowering at the captain. "I'm the only honest man aboard. I'll tell the truth, whatever may come of it. This ship's a slaver. The captain's a murderer and the crew are all thieves. This very night we were to load on the slaves. I know the spot, too, where we were heading to pick them up!"

"You were listening at the cabin door!" the slave captain shouted. "Double-crossing rat!"

"I know what every man aboard knows," said the cook truculently. "But the rest won't talk."

"You've talked enough now!"

The Spanish gentleman, cursing, whipped out a knife and lunged at the informer. The cook staggered, snarling with pain. Blood dripped from his shoulder as he tried to choke his assailant. Two sailors tried to pull them apart. As if this were a signal, the rest of the slaver's crew tried to rush *Old Ironsides'* men.

A general scuffle followed. But the desperate resistance put up by the slavers did not help their case. The captain was clapped into handcuffs, the Spanish gentleman looked considerably mussed, and the whole gang, except the cook, was taken aboard the *Constitution* and put in the brig for safekeeping. The cook had been wounded by the Spanish gentleman's knife, but not so seriously that he could not continue giving his vital bit of evidence.

With armed sailors and some Marines aboard her, the *Gambrill* kept her midnight appointment at a dark and lonely cove. Sure enough, the loading pen was there — a heavily guarded stockade crammed with weeping, groaning, miserable human beings, bound hand and foot, helplessly awaiting their fate.

The half-dozen white men who guarded it took to the woods. One was captured; the rest got away. But the ringleaders were already safe in the *Constitution*'s brig.

The terrified slaves were freed. They were not turned back into the jungles, where the same fate might await them again, but were put aboard a vessel bound for the free state of Liberia. Thus one shipload of slaves never did reach its destination, and one cargo of "ebony" was saved from the black market in slaves.

The *Gambrill* was *Old Ironsides'* only capture on this frustrating cruise. She was a flagship virtually without a fleet, although the British squadron had increased its ships and added some small steam vessels. There were 3,000 miles of West African coastline to patrol. Malaria was a constant hazard. Men were often ill.

At home, the country was on the verge of the Civil War. It was as though the African squadron had been deliberately neglected by a Congress still bitterly divided over slavery. But this changed after Secession, for President Lincoln lost no time in commissioning more ships to help break up the slave trade.

If the *Gambrill* was the *Constitution*'s only capture on this assignment, it was also her last; she was never again used for active service. After the Civil War ships of her type became obsolete. Wooden vessels no longer commanded the seas. The proud and beautiful ship had become an antiquity.

CHAPTER XV

The Last Big Crossing

"$\mathscr{A}$ND HAS IT come to this, old girl, that the thieves have made you a coffin ship, bound to sink us any minute?"

The old sailor spoke sorrowfully into the night. There was no one to hear him. A howling black wind snatched the words from his mouth and carried them off to sea with a wild shriek. Bracing himself against the tossing deck and the stinging slap of spray, he clutched his oilskins tighter about him and lapsed into a lonely reverie.

He could hear the groaning of the ship laboring in the darkness — an almost human sound. Everything rocked, creaked, strained. Old timber, rotted with time. Planks coming apart at the seams. A leak sprung in midocean. The pumps working day and night to keep her clear.

"It's eighty-one years old you are now," the old sailor continued sorrowfully, speaking to the ship as to a beloved friend. "We've grown old together, you and I."

Mike Loughlin, a seamed and weatherbeaten veteran of sailing vessels, remembered the days of his youth. Thirty-five years ago he had shipped on *Old Ironsides* and kept watch on this very deck, and Skipper Mad Jack had had him beaten for skulking. He had been a lad of eighteen then, adventurous and fun-loving, full of the wonder of the sea and of far places. Ah, how the sea had battered him about since then! And now he was an old salt, a kind fast disappearing from the sea. The kind that knew how to climb up the ratlines in the dark and reef a tops'l in a gale. The kind no longer needed about a steamer's deck. Times had changed.

The ship ploughed through the mid-Atlantic gale.

How gallantly she struggled, thought Mike Loughlin. Like the old days. But she carried a heavy burden. Almost a thousand tons of freight — *freight*, if you please! Her decks were stripped of her historic old guns. Huge crates crowded her spar deck with trolley cars, a locomotive, and other examples of the rising Age of Steam for the world's fair in Paris, the Exposition of 1879.

So it had come to this. Mike Loughlin sighed. "A coffin ship. A ferryboat freighter. Headed — who knows? Perhaps for Davy Jones, steam engine, street-cars, and all!"

At the helm, four men clung to the wheel, trying to hold it steadily on course. The lieutenant of the watch came by with a lantern, making the rounds. A sudden roll flung the old sailor and the young lieutenant into each other's arms. They clung to one another like wrestlers, swaying and stumbling.

"Steady — steady now, old girl!" said Mike Loughlin to himself. The ship seemed to take a deep breath; she righted herself and sped onward like a racehorse.

"The wind never yet blew that could knock her down!" the lieutenant shouted exultantly above the wind. "But how I'd like to get my hands on the thieves that stole her repair money!"

Mike Loughlin nodded. Coffin ship!

The money appropriated for the historic frigate had certainly not been properly spent on her. She had received a botched job, a few patches here and there. For many a year she had been in retirement as a training ship and had not smelled salt water. And now she was in no proper shape to put to sea. Worst of all, she had run into the severest weather of many a season in crossing the Atlantic.

For all this, the gallant old ship safely made the crossing. Captain Oscar Badger thanked his lucky star and the famous luck of the ship, and telegraphed to Washington: "Arrived Havre. Unloading freight for Paris exhibits."

The port of Le Havre was crowded with steamships and sailing vessels flying almost every flag known under the sun. Ships of every nation arrived each day, bringing exhibits for the fair. Here the *Constitution* remained at anchor for nine long and tedious months, waiting to take the American exhibits home when the fair closed.

Crowds came to her wharf to see the man-of-war of bygone days — not only the French people, but visiting dignitaries of many other lands who had come to Paris for the exposition. Russians, Japanese, Siamese — in the most faraway places people knew of *Old Ironsides* and her famous battles. Perhaps the old ship knew this would be her last journey to foreign ports. Perhaps she drank in the color and bustle and the sound of many tongues, happy with it all even though her sailors became bored with the long inactivity, often went off on sprees, and had to be brought back by gendarmes.

At last the time came to pack up and leave for home. The leak had been repaired, and the frigate had undergone a thorough refitting during her long confinement in port. Still, old wood cannot be made sound again. Captain Badger had a few misgivings about crossing the rough Atlantic in the dead of winter, the worst of all possible times. But he trusted to the luck of the ship. Besides, he had orders to sail at once. Whatever could be done had been done. Seams had been caulked carefully. Gunports had been sealed tight. She was finally ready.

The *Constitution* left France in a snowstorm and

headed into the English Channel. She sailed on a Friday — and that, said old-timers, meant that anything could happen. It was an ancient superstition that Friday was a day of ill luck. It almost seemed as if there might be some truth in it. The turbulent Channel crossing was a threat of more to come.

At midnight the lieutenant made the rounds and wrote in the log: "At sea. Overcast, windy, cold. Ship making headway."

All seemed well.

At 2:00 A.M. she headed into a heavy bank of fog. Nothing unusual in these parts. But the lieutenant peered into darkness. Somehow he had the feeling that something was wrong.

He listened intently. That sinister, hissing sound . . . Waves breaking — surf rolling on a beach! The ship was in the midst of breakers!

"Hard down!" he yelled to the helmsman. "Put her down fast! And hold her, though your arms tear out of their sockets!"

The helmsman jammed the wheel over hard. A grinding sound made the lieutenant grit his teeth and brace himself for the shock. But the ship struck without undue violence. She jolted to a stop less than her own length away from a looming two-hundred-foot cliff!

For the first time in her life, *Old Ironsides* had run aground and barely escaped wreckage. She was fast stuck somewhere off the famous chalk cliffs of Dover. Thank heaven she had picked a spot where there were no large rocks to rip out her hull.

Her crew braced everything flat aback and set the mizzen topgallant sail while the ship settled to leeward. Then they fired the guns and rockets to signal their distress. All night the frigate waited, settling further on her side. Heavy surf battered her.

At daybreak three British tugs steamed toward her. They huffed and puffed and failed to budge her an inch. The water casks were emptied, her bilge was pumped out, and the ballast was heaved into the sea to lighten her.

She was listing badly when a fourth and then a fifth tug came to help. They strained together at full speed. A grating sound came along the old ship's keel, and she suddenly floated clear on the high tide.

In Portsmouth, England, she had to go into drydock to determine how much damage had been done to her hull. The British patched her again, and she set out on her last lap.

The ship's log recorded her passage across the Atlantic:

> February 9, 1879. Squally, lightning. Made ready for squalls.
>
> February 10, 1879. Squally and threatening.

February 11, 1879. Squally, misty, changeable.

February 13, 1879. Fresh breeze to strong gales.
Frequent heavy thumps caused by seas striking stern
and rudder. Frequent heavy squalls and rains.

The frightened helmsman suddenly found that the
ship would not answer to the wheel. She spun about,
sails slatting, completely out of control. Her masts
pitched and tossed as she wallowed helplessly in heavy
seas.

Throughout the ship the crew heard a strange knocking, a loud, hollow thumping like the pounding of a
drum. The noise came from the stern. They found that
the ship's rudder had broken off in the storm! *Old Ironsides* was now drifting rudderless somewhere at sea in a
heavy gale.

The broken rudder still hung loosely at the stern,
fastened by rudder chains and heavy hawsers. It was
causing the violent thumping, as the waves twisted it
back and forth and slammed it against the stern. Not
only was the rudder a useless appendage now; it had
become a source of great peril. By its wild movements
it was flinging the ship about with such violent motions
that she was beyond any control of her sails, and in great
danger.

Now the gunports were awash. The masts pitched
horizontally and almost went under. The loud, empty

knocking further unnerved everyone. Large crates broke from their moorings and careened about the hold, a new threat to the ship's safety.

The captain decided that the broken rudder must be cut loose and cast adrift. Then, at least, they could try to steady the ship with her sails until help came or they managed to make the nearest port. He called for volunteers to go over the stern and cut the fastenings. It was a dangerous job.

Three men stepped forward and offered to make the attempt. They armed themselves with axes, ropes, saws, and lanterns and vanished over the bucking stern in a whirl of sleet, howling wind, and blinding spray.

Those on deck peered anxiously over the rail. The three men tossed below, clinging to icy ropes, and chopped and hacked at the rudder moorings. Three storm lanterns fastened to their belts swung and bobbed about with them as they worked. Now and then their voices carried on the wind, calling out orders or advice to one another or reporting progress to the deck. At last they managed to cut the hawsers, sever the chains, and cast the broken rudder clear of the ship. The terrible thumping stopped at once, and the men clambered aboard.

Almost within reach of safety, one of the three lost his grip on the icy rope to which he was clinging and fell, plummeting with his lantern into the sea. Someone shouted "Man overboard!" and the crew rushed to the boats to try to save him. Numbed and shivering, his two mates were hauled up on deck, but the third man could not be saved. On those violently tossing seas it was impossible to launch a boat and look for him; it would be smashed to splinters before they could even get it down.

In vain his shipmates leaned over the rail, peering at the spot where his lantern had vanished and calling into the gray murk: "Mike! Mike Loughlin! Ahoy! Aho-o-o-oy there!"

There was no answer from Mike Loughlin, and no trace of him that anyone could see.

Captain Badger managed to bring his disabled ship safely through several more stormbeaten days. He put in at Lisbon, where the remains of the broken rudder were examined. The material was so rotten that it was no wonder it had crumbled at sea!

The Portuguese built a new rudder, and the frigate reached home this time without further incident — nothing worse, anyway, than a four-hour spell at the pumps for the crew every day, to keep her dry.

And that was the last crossing *Old Ironsides* ever made.

They say that before their heads go under, drowning men see things that are hidden from others. At least, that is one of the many superstitions of the sea. Did Mike Loughlin see, over the frigate's high black wall, a crowd of ghostly figures at her rail?

Mad Jack shaking his black whalebone cane.

Isaac Hull thundering and stomping about.

Preble waving his sword and thundering at his "boys."

Decatur, with tousled hair, staring out to sea.

All the old sea captains, some good and some bad, who walked her quarter-deck. And many others, too — small boys and brawny men, white sailors and black. Ghosts of a gaudy, brutal, brave, adventurous era: the vanished days of sail.

Afterword

$\mathcal{B}$ECAUSE THIS story unfolds through such a long stretch of time it could not have one main character, except, of course, for *Old Ironsides* herself. A small boy who might have enlisted on the frigate *Constitution*'s first cruise would have been a gray-haired old salt if he had sailed around the world with Skipper "Mad Jack," and would be approaching a century when the historic ship crossed the seas for the last time.

History cannot be changed. We have records of all the great battles, the chases and captures, the historic events in which the *Constitution* played her part. Therefore, the main events which form the background of the story are true. Against that background, characters — some real, some imaginary — interact with each other. We know the names of the *Constitution*'s officers: the commodores, captains, lieutenants and midshipmen, and usually something about the way they looked and spoke and how they behaved in these great events. We can try to imagine them more clearly and to eavesdrop on what they might have said under certain circumstances.

As for the ordinary sailors, the thousands of men and boys, they are for the most part unknown to us. Therefore Johnny Griggs, Jethro Stubbs, Amos Brown, Long Tom, Bill Fergusson, and Mike Loughlin are imaginary characters. They were called out of the mists of imagination to take the places of people who lived through so much history and adventure but left no personal records. Moses Smith did write his memoirs, and other sailors on different cruises kept journals and even published them, but this was rather rare.

It is hoped that, by telling the story in this way, a romantic period in American history has been made vivid for the reader; and that the reader may experience what life was like on the decks of *Old Ironsides* when she rode the high seas so long ago.